# ALIENESE

## Oliver Davis Pike

Arachis Press 2019

Alienese
©2019 Oliver Davis Pike

ISBN 978-1-937745-62-2

Arachis Press
4803 Peanut Road
Graceville, FL 32440
http://arachispress.com

# PART I. ORBITING

## Chapter 1

"THE LARNAGIANS WON'T like this at all," said Nok, holding up his device so his companion could see the reading. "No, not at all."

The other touched it with a tentacle. "Isn't that just too bad?"

So the aliens were capable of sarcasm. I had wondered about that, as I had about many things. Some aliens, anyway; these two were of quite different races and, I assumed, different planets.

"Can you let me in on it?" I asked. Damn, I wished I understood what those stares meant. An alien language I had learned quickly enough. Alien body-language was another matter.

"We'd better not," said the companion. As its name was completely unpronounceable, I just thought of it as Nok's companion. Or as Squid, in that it looked a bit like one. Only a bit.

"We have a Larnagian aboard," Nok explained. "They're necessary, you know."

"He doesn't know," pointed out Squid. "And the Larnagian should not know about you, kid. If it did, its whole planet might come and wipe out your whole planet. Believe me."

"So forget we tested you," added Nok.

"And that you passed."

"We'll have to check out more of them," Nok told his companion. "Dave could be an aberration."

The squid spoke as gravely as possible, considering its squeak of a voice, "We could dissect him and maybe figure out what makes him work." By now I recognized the ear-piercing whistles that followed as the being's version of laughter.

Nok twitched his antennae. *That* I had figured out was equivalent to a shrug of the shoulders or maybe even a shake of the head. Neither of which Nok had. "So what is a Larnagian?" I asked. "I've only seen, um, crewmen who look like you two."

"Larnagians navigate," said Squid. "They allow us to move from star to star."

Hmm. "I thought that was impossible."

"It is," admitted Nok, "for everyone but Larnagians." He then gave me a long look. Why, I had no idea.

"I need a drink," said Squid. "Let's sample some more Earth booze."

"The last made you sick," Nok pointed out.

"They put some kind of poison berries in it. What'd you call them, Dave?"

"Juniper. Better stick to vodka."

Nok's antennae twitched again. "That we can get at home. We know how to make pure alcohol, my boy!"

"It's the exotic stuff we want to sample. What does this label say?"

"Bourbon. It's another kind of whiskey." They had already tried whiskeys.

"Bourbon," repeated the Squid. "Bourbon. I like the name." It poured out three beakers. "So much to research!"

"It's good to be a scientist," stated Nok. He took the proffered beaker in one of his four hands, sniffed at its contents. Or waved his antennae back and forth above it, which was the equivalent of sniffing. "Not burnt like the last one."

"Smoky," came Squid's correction. "It was smoky and I liked it." Three straw-like mouths sipped at the liquor. "Disappointing."

Nok apparently did not agree. "Almost like a good flurgal."

"Maybe," admitted Squid. "Further testing is needed." It refilled their beakers.

"And not just of booze," added Nok. He gave me — their guest

4

or maybe their captive — another looking over. "Should we put Dave back or take him with us?"

"Up to the captain but I'll recommend bringing him along. You don't mind, do you, kid?"

I was about to tell him I did when Nok said, "Not permanently. A year or two might pass on your planet."

"I suppose that would be okay. As long as you don't carry through on the dissection idea." I did hope that was no more than a joke.

"Not unless you die," promised Squid. "Are there any other kinds of smoky booze?"

"Besides scotch? Not that I know of." Which admittedly didn't mean much. "We do have all sorts of smoked foods."

Squid made some sort of gesture with the tentacles. I could only assume it meant something. "Too dangerous. They're likely to be poison to us."

"Liquor is generally safe."

"Unless poison berries are added," Squid pointed out. "Hmm, maybe this bourbon isn't so bad. Bourbon, bourbon, bourbon."

"Boor-bon?" A stranger walked into the lab. Yes, actually walked. For a moment I thought the newcomer was a fellow human.

Only for a moment. But it *was* sort of humanoid, with a pair each of arms and legs, as well as a head. Some strange sort of skin — no, idiot, I told himself, those are clothes! A coverall.

"Want a sample, Wani?" asked Nok.

"I thought you'd never ask." It turned its eyes on me. "Interesting. Almost larnagoid."

"As are a number of species on a number of planets," stated Squid.

"True enough. You guys are the scientists. Hey, this is good stuff," said Wani, tasting the bourbon. "We need to put this planet on the trade routes."

"After a couple decades going through the bureaucratic gears," said Nok.

"Or centuries," amended Squid. "An opportunity for a little off-the-books trade, maybe?"

"But you didn't hear it here," added Nok, topping off the visitor's beaker.

Wani gave me an even longer looking over, nodded in a most human manner, drained the whiskey, and left.

"That's a Larnagian, I assume."

Squid whistled. "So it is. Since everyone else on this ship looks like Nok or me, it was a pretty safe guess."

"I think she was trying to decide whether one of her kind could slip onto your planet and do a little smuggling without attracting notice. She does look a lot like a human."

If one ignored the ape-like face and whatever else might be under that jumpsuit. Not my concern, at least not right then.

Squid finished the last of its bourbon too. "That will dry me out, as usual. I'd better go submerge and sleep a while," it said. "Bye guys." It swayed a bit as it rolled out of the room.

"We might as well get out of this lab too," spoke Nok. "I'll walk you to your quarters." They always walked me to my quarters — which were locked — so I wouldn't get into any sort of trouble. What trouble I could get into, I had no idea. It might be interesting to find out sometime.

I said Squid looks like a squid, but only sort-of. That's because of the tentacles. Its body is more like a three-armed star fish, supporting the squiddy part, the tentacles, the mouths, the eyes, all in multiples of three. There were more squid-stars aboard, scuttling about on those three thick legs and all looking pretty much the same to me.

Then I saw one in the passageway that didn't look the same. "What happened to it?" I whispered to Nok. "Injury?"

"Just had sex," he whispered back. "They lose a leg in the process."

The individual we were whispering about had two normal legs plus a tiny one. "It's regenerating it?"

"Yep. Astute of you, Dave. Each partner gives up a lobe of its body to form a new individual. Than all three generate new legs to be whole again."

Oh. I wondered if it felt good but decided it best not to ask. And I definitely was not going to quiz Nok about his own sex life. For all I knew that caterpillar-like body might turn into a butterfly. What I did ask was, "Then your companion is, um, asexual?"

"One of the few intelligent species to be so. The two sex paradigm is by far the most common in the universe. Speaking of which —" Nok hesitated and then let it all out in a rush. "We intend to bring another of your species aboard. Would you prefer male or female?"

"It doesn't matter." And it didn't. Chances were I wouldn't get along with either.

# Chapter 2

THE LANGUAGE I had learned, with the help of mysterious electronic devices, was a simple one, a pidgin, used by many races from many worlds. So I had been told by the technician who hooked me up to those mysterious electronic devices. She was of Nok's race. As they wore no sort of coverings and their sexual organs were in plain view, I had no problem identifying her as female and Nok as male.

That did not mean they would act anything like human males and females. Not that one could trust human males and females to act like human males and females.

I was ignored most of the next day. I had a clock so I knew it was a day — a shipboard day, which seemed close enough to one at home. Home. What was 'home' now? My empty house? My planet? This stinky spaceship?

Yes, it did stink. Don't think I got used to that low tide smell that seemed to cling to everything.

Nok and Squid came to visit me, late. "We have more humans," Nok announced.

"We chose specimens from your own culture. No point in putting up extra barriers."

"Right. Two females. They're being processed now."

"Two?"

"They were together so it seemed simpler to bring both," said Squid.

Nok added, "They might have been lost in the wilderness. Females shouldn't be allowed to wander away from home!"

Maybe I was right about the females of Nok's home not being like humans. Or maybe it was just Nok's view of things. I'd known human men who might have said something of the same sort.

"The females on this ship seem to have wandered far from home," I pointed out.

Nok had no answer. Squid whistled.

"So does this mean you're ready to leave?" I asked.

"Not yet," said Squid. "We're going to lurk in your system a little longer. Lots to study but we have to make an end of it sometime."

Nok wiggled his antennae. "And make a report of it."

"And then decide whether to put you back or take you along. All three or any one of you. Hey, kid, would you like to get a look at the newcomers?"

"Sure," I told it. Squid fussed with the controls on the viewer. The last time I tried that I only succeeded in turning it off and couldn't get it to come back on. So I hadn't been watching anything.

"Try the language lab," said Nok. Sure enough, there they were, both of them. Yep, women. They'd got that right. Youngish. Younger than me, anyway. They looked like blank-faced idiots at the moment, as they got their magic language lessons. I've no doubt I looked worse.

They were nude too. Probably just a part of their processing but I felt too voyeuristic watching them, and looked away. "I'll meet them eventually?"

"Tomorrow," said Squid. "Maybe."

"We'll watch, of course," admitted Nok. "And take lots of notes." He turned to Squid. "Do you think we'll see fear or relief?"

"Both," I told him. Not just from the women.

These two would be watching me just as closely as their new subjects. I glanced back at the screen, despite myself. "Pale," I commented. Most of them — the faces and hands were a bit tanned.

Nok made some kind of note on his recorder. "Is that attractive to human males?" he asked.

I could only shrug. "To some, I am sure." All women are attractive, I could have said. Especially when they are the only ones for thousands of miles. But they did have ugly haircuts.

"It's been a long day," said Squid, reaching a tentacle out and switching the screen off. "We gathered some new samples of booze, too. What say we go over to the lab and, um, catalog them?"

"The ones labeled 'wine' look interesting. You know anything about them, Dave?"

"I know they are made from fruit and might give our friend a tummy-ache," I informed him.

"Ah," said Squid. "The sacrifices we must make in the name of science!"

# Chapter 3

"YOU'VE LEARNED TO speak Alienese, I would guess," I said to the pair, "but English might be more comfortable for all of us." And annoy Nok and Squid.

I had entered their room as openly as possible, spreading my hands in what I hoped was a universal sign of good intentions. Maybe I looked like I was about to bless them.

"Okay," replied the taller one. Canadian accent? Or upper Midwest, anyway. "So who are you?"

"Dave Ladd's the name. I've been aboard a couple weeks. Hmm, close to three, I guess."

The short, slightly plump one squinted at me. "The musician?"

A fan? That was a rarity anywhere. "So I claim."

She turned to her friend. "He wrote that sexist song I hate."

Oh. "Whichever one it was, I have more of them," I informed her. "I was on my way to a gig when my van broke down on a back road in Alabama." I shrugged in as self-deprecating a manner as I could muster and said, "And ended up here."

Both were in jeans and flannel shirts. Hiking boots rested on the floor. They must have been backpacking. "We were backpacking," said the tall one. "Up in the Chippewa Forest. I'm Donna."

So our alien friends had again chosen humans who could disappear without too much fuss being raised. "I'm Mickie," said the other. "Who grabbed us, anyway? You're the first human being we've seen."

"And the only one you're likely to see. The alien who processed you is a Sormog. I just think of them as the caterpillar people and the others here as squid-star people. I can't pronounce the name of the squid-star planet."

"Does it revolve around the Squid Star?" asked Donna. She kept a straight face but her tone gave her away.

"I wouldn't be surprised." Two could play at that. "Before I go on let me say that I have no idea what they plan to do with you. With us. They say they might put us back."

"And wipe our memories?" asked Mickie.

"I think that only happens on tee-vee," said Donna, but she gave me a questioning look anyway.

"And I think you're right." But I didn't know for sure, did I? "They do recognize us as sentient beings and won't mistreat us. I have a fair amount of faith in this."

"I hope they don't expect us to breed," piped up Mickie.

"Yeah," I laughed, "I've already figured out that isn't going to work. Hmm, you should be aware that they're likely to observe you. And definitely record you. Just a heads-up."

"Oh," said Donna, "we can make porn for aliens!" She snickered. "Or with aliens!"

Mickie said nothing but did redden considerably. Maybe Donna embarrassed her frequently. People will put up with things for love, won't they? "Not with the squid-stars," I told her. "They don't have sexes." But they did have sex of a sort.

"Not with anyone or anything," Mickie stated quite firmly. She almost glared at me.

"Of course, my love. Are we going to get fed, Dave?"

"Sure. They have to steal stuff from Earth since their food would probably poison us." How much would need to be stockpiled if Nok and Squid carried all of us off to other worlds? I had no idea how long a trip might last but they had mentioned the possibility of years.

The door had shut behind me. I wondered if it was locked. Yep. "Hey guys," I called out in the pidgin, "why don't you let me out so the gir — um, women can settle in? We can all get to know each other better tomorrow."

"Okay," came Nok's reply. "I'll just — which one of these opens it?" he mumbled.

"That one," came Squid's distinct squeak.

"Right." A moment later the lock clanked and I was able to turn the latch.

"I reckon I'll be seeing you," I told the two women. Whether I wanted to or not. "I wouldn't worry much about all this. Not now, anyway." With that I stepped out into the narrow hallway.

Was that the Larnagian hurrying off the other direction? A squid-star I didn't know was holding two paper bags. "For the specimens," it said, and handed them to me.

I sniffed but it wasn't necessary. One could see the fast-food logo on the sides. "They seem to have sent down to Earth to get you some supper," I announced and handed over the bags. "You're taking me back to my room?" I asked the squid-star.

"To the lab," it replied and turned, lumbering down the hall on its three stout legs. I followed. Squid and Nok awaited me. I think they were eager but it's never easy to tell.

"Where did the burgers come from?" I asked.

Nok answered. "Wani popped down to the planet to get them. Larnagians can do that."

Without a ship? I realized I knew nothing of Larnagians. It might be good to change that. At least learn the secret I was supposed to be keeping from them. "That wouldn't be convenient, long-term," I pointed out.

"Nor would our Larnagian be willing," he replied. "So, how did you like the females? Do you think you might mate?"

"Unlikely. They are lesbians."

"Lesbians?" He poked at the device he carried. "Oh, homosexuals. Excellent! A different angle from which to look at your race."

"I would have liked to see them mate, though," said Squid. It almost sounded wistful.

"We'll organize a field trip," his comrade promised. "I'm sure someone somewhere on Earth is mating."

"Most likely," I agreed.

"But we bring no more humans aboard. We bent the rules with three of them."

"It's necessary," objected Squid. "We needed a good sample size."

"And we'll do some testing on our field trip to increase that sample size. Now," said Nok, "what do we do about poor Dave here? He must be disappointed!"

"Not so much," I told him. "It makes things simpler." In fact, Donna and Mickie might be the perfect companions. Donna, anyway. I wasn't sure Mickie liked me much.

"Wani didn't bring anything for me, did she?"

"She did. Then she ate them herself. What were those called?"

"Donuts. She liked them a whole lot and, ah, I do not think they are going to upset her at all."

"Neither do I," said Nok. "Neither do I."

I didn't see much point in asking why. Also, I knew where the fridge was in the lab so I helped myself to some of the ice cream they had brought up a few days ago. Unfortunately, spoons were not part of the lab equipment so I had to eat it with my fingers.

"Trying out anything new tonight?" I asked.

"We'll never find anything to match the saki we sampled last night," declared Nok. "The Sormogian market would take all your planet could produce."

"And they are welcome to it," Squid said.

Saki would be a good investment if I ever made it back. I'd have to remember that. Maybe liquor in general. From listening to these two, Earth didn't have much else to offer the galaxy.

"You know what would be good over this?" I asked, holding up my bowl. "Some schnapps. Have you guys tried that yet?"

# Chapter 4

BOTH THESE ALIEN scientists were generalists of a sort. On a small survey ship, that worked best. There were some hard science individuals aboard too, geologists and such, but I did not interact with any of those. Nok was the equivalent of an anthropologist, maybe. Squid was more biology oriented.

That meant Squid oversaw our diet. "I'll have to go with nutrition dense food once we leave this system," he told me. "There is only so much space."

"But we need some fiber in our diet too," I informed him. "It keeps things moving along inside us."

"Oh? Yes, yes, I should have known, with that long digestive tract of yours. All we X-screech-Z-gulp-screech-ians (I told you it was unpronounceable) have is the one stomach pouch. Well then, fiber. Will sawdust do?"

"Get oatmeal. You should be able to pack plenty of oatmeal in here somewhere and it doesn't need refrigeration or any of that." After all, they carried plenty of provisions for squid-stars and Sormogs. A little extra for humans shouldn't be a problem, should it?

"You know," Nok put in, "they can probably eat the same diet as, um, you-know-who."

"True," agreed Squid. Did the pair think I didn't know who they meant? After all, only one other race was represented on this ship.

"Are the others coming?" I asked.

"Tok is bringing them."

"Tok?" Did I know who that was?

"The technician who taught you all our language," explained Squid.

"What you called Alienese," added Nok. "I think that is a joke, right?"

"More or less." He made some sort of note of it on his ever-present device.

So, the female Sormog. She had never accompanied me anywhere, which helped explain why I didn't know her name. I usually got one squid-star or another.

The three of them were chatting like old friends when they entered. "We should demand our release," stated Donna at once.

"If you insist," said Squid. "Dave never asked."

"All this was too interesting. I couldn't help think of what I might miss if you put me back." Back in a worn-out van and a worn-out career.

"He's right," said Mickie. "We'd be passing up an adventure."

Donna laughed, a bit raucously. "I never thought asking would work! But maybe you're right. This *is* too good to pass up. We'll stay, Squiddo."

"We may yet put you all back when we leave," Nok told her. "It isn't decided yet."

"We haven't been gone long. No one would be likely to know anything had even happened," Mickie said, and turned to me. "How 'bout you?"

"Someone might have noticed I was gone." But they might not have cared. "I assume my van would have been found."

"Um, no," spoke up Tol. "It's packed away for further study."

"I wasn't aware of that," Nok said. The way his antenna stood up was an indication of pique, I had decided. I could have been wrong.

"Gof asked for it."

"Oh, Gof," said Squid. "He loves to take things apart."

"But he should have asked. All artifacts are my concern,"

maintained Nok. "Still, it simplifies matters when it comes to Dave's disappearance."

It did — if I was put back on Earth now. Ha, I could even claim I had been abducted by aliens and no one would much care. "Not if I'm gone for a year or more."

"Same here," said Donna. "I do have a job and stuff."

"Which you're always threatening to quit. I'm all for exploring the universe," declared her girlfriend.

"Me too," I admitted. Why not?

Donna shrugged. "Me three."

"We'll advise the captain to keep you," promised Squid. "It's up to it."

"Then we can get to testing." Nok began fussing with a box of some sort, with the usual switches and dials. It was finished in a nausea-inducing lustrous greenish color. These aliens did not see things quite the same as humans. Nok's 'eyes' barely looked like eyes, more like large glossy black patches on his skin. Photo-receptors of some sort, I guessed, but that's about as far as my scientific knowledge went.

"That?" asked Squid. "Let's get right to the genetics."

Nok glanced toward Tol, involuntarily maybe. These guys weren't good at hiding things — and they were definitely hiding things. "Not yet," he said. He bent over the device, his long body in the usual 'S' shape he assumed when working or resting. It formed more of a 'L' when he moved about. If that Sormogian shape were straightened out it would be a couple feet longer than me, but it had never straightened out so far. Maybe when he slept or whatever a Sormog did.

Even bent, he was taller than Squid, who came about to my waist. Tol, incidentally, was bigger than Nok. Maybe that was true of Sormog females in general. I'd have to see more of them to know.

"Mickie, right?" asked Nok. "Stand over there if you will and let me scan you."

"Checking for parasites and that sort of thing," explained Squid.

It took only a couple minutes to scan both women. "Mmm, yes, reasonably clean," decided Nok. "Pretty much the same bacteria and viruses we found in Dave. And neither pregnant."

"I would hope not," commented Donna. She squinted at Tol. "Does that sort of thing happen much here?"

I couldn't read the rapid waving of the Sormog's antennae. Maybe she was embarrassed. Squid spoke up. "Mostly to my people. It doesn't take us very long."

Nok had no comment on the subject and, in fact, changed the subject. "Or course, it is extremely unlikely that we could contract any sort of disease from you humans. Our biology is far too different."

"But it's best to be careful," said Squid. The two stared at each other a moment — I could recognize their stares. There was something else to this, something they were not going to tell us.

They spent some time fussing about with other instruments. It looked like busywork to me, wasting time as long as Tol was present. "That is enough for now, don't you think?" asked Nok eventually.

"Yes," agreed Squid. "We should correlate all this. Tol, will you accompany the female humans back to their quarters, please? Um, maybe you should go too, Dave."

We were not too far down the hall before the Sormog commented, "I wish they weren't being so secretive. Don't they think I understand things?"

"Just like men," asserted Mickie.

"Only one is a man. Male, I should say," I told her. "And I don't think they are sharing with anyone, Tol."

"They will have to, sooner or later. Here's the room."

We all went in but I informed her, "The women's room, not mine."

Her antennae waved about. "I don't have time to take you there. Stay with them." With that she slid out. The door closed behind her. I was pretty sure it locked too.

# Chapter 5

"She's steamed," said Donna.

Mildly miffed, I would have said. But I didn't. "I guess you're stuck with me till they want us in the lab again."

Mickie snickered. "Or you're stuck with us. Those whatevers — scientists?" I nodded. "They *were* reluctant about something, weren't they?"

"If they've learned something interesting about us they might want to save it," felt Donna. "You know, make a big announcement when they get home."

"Entirely possible," I said. I doubted it but it really was possible.

"Or maybe Nok is just a big dick," said Mickie. "They do look like giant dicks. We're on a spaceship full of dicks and squids." She snickered again and pushed back the brown-blond hair that had flopped across her eyes.

"I think I'll stick with Dave's caterpillar description," replied Donna.

"Nok does have a dick. I saw it," continued Mickie, apparently not ready to give up the topic. "A dick with a dick."

"And maybe some other Sormog somewhere appreciates it," Donna said. "Is it time for lunch yet?"

"I hope we don't get fast food again."

That seemed unlikely to me. "Last night was the first time I've seen any here." Mostly, I ate in the lab. Nok and Squid had taken notes on it at first. "The navigator brought it. You haven't seen her yet but she's a different species from the others."

"She doesn't look like a dick, does she?"

Donna shook her head and then giggled. "Hey, maybe she'll look like a vagina!"

"I'm afraid not. Maybe you'll see her around." Though it had taken three weeks before I caught my first glimpse of Wani.

Mickie fiddled with the controls to the viewer. She had better luck with it than I, but the image on the screen was nothing but an empty hallway. "Do you know what any of these symbols mean, Ladd?" she asked.

"No idea," I admitted.

Donna wondered, "Why didn't they teach us that along with the language?"

"Afraid we'd get in trouble, maybe." Not maybe. Probably. We remained wild animals of a sort.

"Well, then I'll guess," announced Mickie. "Oh, isn't that Tol?"

I wasn't sure I'd recognize the differences between her and any other female Sormog, but it was her lab. "I think so."

She was curled up in a spiral. So that was how they slept.

"That's not so interesting." She ran a finger across the control panel and a different scene appeared. Space. And that little orb there was Earth.

"Damn," said Donna. I agreed.

"I'm not so sure I want to stay now," whispered Mickie.

I wondered if we were being observed. Recorded, for sure. One would forget that fact after a time. I needed to keep reminding myself.

"Imagine seeing another planet like that," I said. "A planet revolving around another star."

"I think I want to see that."

"Me, too," said Donna.

Yeah, me three.

The door slid open to reveal a squid-star. I thought it might be the one who brought food last night. There were differences between individuals and I was starting to notice them. "I am to accompany you to the laboratory," it stated. "There will be food."

"Then lead on, MacSquid," said Donna.

"My name is ZD-chortle-chortle-XX-squeal," it announced, as we trooped out behind it. "What is a macsquid?"

"A term of respect," I told it. "And you probably know we can't pronounce your name."

"I have trouble with it myself. MacSquid is acceptable." We were there. "I'll wait outside," said MacSquid. The lab door slid closed behind us.

"I think I like MacSquid," Donna said, apparently directing her remark to Squid and Nok. "Can you assign him to us permanently?"

"It," Nok told her. "It is an it, and if it and the captain are willing, certainly."

"So what's for lunch?" I asked.

"Oatmeal," replied Squid. "As you suggested."

It was dry and uncooked, three bowls full. Fortunately, I had kitchen privileges in the lab. "Raisins would be a good addition," I told them as the water heated. "Some brown sugar, too."

"Or just stock up on boxes of Granola," said Mickie.

"Granola," Squid said into its recorder.

Nok had a device of his own in one of his hands and was waving it about, nearer and farther from the women, and checking the readings frequently. "Yes, the genetics are the same," he stated.

"We should check some more individuals down on the planet to confirm."

"To be sure, but I doubt these three are all aberrations."

"It would seem unlikely," agreed Squid. "Oatmeal needs to be cooked," he told his recording device. "With added ingredients?"

"Not essential but they make it more palatable," I told him.

Mickie made an exaggerated face. "Donna likes onions in hers."

Why not? It sounded like something I might try. Maybe with a couple fried eggs — "I think this is ready."

"Smells interesting," said Nok, twitching his antennae toward the gruel as I portioned it out. "Do they make oatmeal wine?"

"Not that I've ever heard of. Maybe beer." I wasn't at all sure of that.

"Oh, beer," spoke up Donna. "Be sure to stock up on beer! Will it be a long trip?"

Nok and Squid looked at each other. The Sormog gave that wave of the antennae I recognized as a shrug. "An extremely short trip," said Squid. "Instantaneous, in fact."

"There's no reason you shouldn't know that."

"It's all the moving around before and after that takes a while."

"And that," said Nok, "means we can pop right back here at any time. If need be."

# Chapter 6

"BUT IT TAKES a Larnagian, I understand," I told my companions.

"What's that? Some kind of machine?" asked Donna.

"The navigator I mentioned earlier. She's a Larnagian."

"And there is only one aboard. That seems iffy."

I had thought so too. Maybe there was some practical reason. Maybe they charged a lot and the ship could only afford one. How should I know?

"Here's your room, Dave," said MacSquid. "Or are you going with the females?"

"I'll stay." Nok and Squid had kept at their tests quite some time, checking and rechecking their new subjects. Long enough that I had to fix another meal for us. Mac made sure I was inside and the door had closed behind me.

I assumed it took Mickie and Donna on to their own quarters then. I had no way of knowing, unless I could figure out the viewer and learn how to tune in the hallway camera. I didn't feel like experimenting with it right then. In fact, all I felt like was sleeping. The bed with which I had been provided was surprisingly comfortable. Who knows how they managed that?

Sleep. It came quickly and left just as quickly. Someone was there. The door hadn't opened and closed, had it? I was sure I would have seen a brief light, the subdued murmur of its mechanism if it had. I fumbled for the illumination control. It was on the wall somewhere near the bed.

"No need for lights," came a soft but slightly harsh voice. "Oh, maybe a little. Point-nine, um, no, point-eight illumination," it said. Immediately a faint light filled the room.

"I didn't know I could do that," I told Wani, for that was my visitor. I had known that as soon as she spoke.

"Now you do. Would you like it brighter?"

"This is fine." She was, as before, clad in some sort of coverall, only head, hands, and feet protruding. The feet were bare. Had she worn shoes before? They were quite human-looking feet. Brown, as were her face and hands.

"Should you be here?" I asked.

"Nope. Completely against the rules. But I turned off all the recording feeds before coming in. No one will notice."

Until tomorrow, when they checked them. It was unlikely anyone looked into my dark room while I slept. Wani sat down on the end of the bed. She did look human, didn't she? But not human, too. Her dark deep-set eyes peered at me from beneath heavy brow ridges, shaded by unruly curling hair that swept back from a low, receding forehead. Wani's tongue slipped out to wet her quite human lips. "You do look a lot like a Larnagian," she said. "What I can see, anyway. How about —" She pulled back the thin sheet. "Oh, yes."

I had, as usual, been sleeping in the nude. They kept it pretty warm in that ship and I had little incentive to be modest around squid-stars and Sormogs. Things had just changed though, hadn't they?

Wani stood and peeled off her jumpsuit. Damn, she looked every bit a woman from the neck down. A little hairier than the norm, to be sure, but nicely shaped, slender, small-breasted. But that head — the jaw was heavy and chinless, the face protruding, ape-like. Prehistoric, that was how she looked. How could such evolve on another planet, at unimaginable distances from Earth?

"Ah, you like me," she said and slipped into bed. Indeed, I did like her. Three times. Kissing was a little strange but I got used to it.

Kissing? Yes, Wani kissed just like a human. She did pretty

much everything just like a human. "I need to go," she whispered eventually. "Maybe again sometime?"

"Alright with me." It must be lonely, I realized, being the only one of her sort on this ship. Shoot, I could say the same about me. The Larnagian pulled on her coverall and was gone without another word.

Without using the door. That was a surprise. But I'm pretty sure I dozed off a while anyway before my door did open. It was MacSquid. "Time to go somewhere, Mac?" I asked.

"Not yet." It went over to the viewer and messed about with the controls. "Working?" it asked the air. I ducked into the closet of a restroom to relieve myself.

"Perfectly," came a high-pitched reply. Another squid-star, somewhere. I was pulling on my shorts as quickly as I might. It felt different having someone watch me, now.

Mac looked around the room. "It smells different in here," it said. "Stinky."

I could only shrug. "This whole ship smells stinky to me. Ready? Lead on, MacSquid." I couldn't help it, you know? I was probably going to say that a lot for a while.

Only Nok and Squid were waiting in the lab. Maybe they wanted to talk to me alone. But first, "Give me some time to clean up. I, um, perspired a lot last night."

"You aren't sick, are you?" asked Squid.

"Nah. I'm gonna need more clothes if we're gone very long. The girls too." Hmm. Yeah, that was an idea. "I bet we could all fit into those jumpsuits like Wani wears."

The shower was open to the main room and not designed nor built for a being my size and shape but I could make do. It might have been intended for emergency use, like laboratory showers on Earth. Quite ordinary water rained on me from a pair of nozzles.

"Easy to procure," noted Nok. "Certainly a better idea than going down to the planet for them. You do have to wear coverings?"

"It's probably a good idea." Especially with the women here. And Wani, for that matter.

"Just like a Larnagian," commented Squid.

"Yes, just. By the way, we officially requested that the three of you come back with us."

"That's not at all unusual. It might help move things along for open contact."

"Which we will recommend," finished Nok.

After further study, no doubt. I knew these two wanted to look us humans over some more. And there would be scientists waiting with the same idea. Suddenly, I felt misgivings about the whole thing.

I dried myself on one of the luxurious towels. I'd never felt one quite so soft. People would gladly trade bourbon or saki or whatever these aliens wanted for them. "There are other races, right?" I asked. "I mean, out there where we're headed. Besides you two and the Larnagians."

"Many. Some travel, some don't. It's convenient to limit a crew to two or three compatible races."

"Plus a Larnagian."

"Of course," said Nok. "Preferably a young female like Wani. They, ah, see more clearly."

Whatever that meant. "And Larnagians can travel from world to world. Without a ship? Is that right?"

"Dave would learn all this soon enough anyway," said Nok. "We might as well fill him in."

"Agreed. Yes, the Larnagians can transport themselves anywhere without a ship but they can also, with a little help from computers, transport a ship. That is, they open the way and the computer can follow it."

"You mean they just *think* it and they are there?"

"So it is, Dave. So it is."

# Chapter 7

"I watched you," Wani admitted. "Ever since I saw you in the lab."

She had appeared in my room before I even fell asleep. 'Again sometime' had apparently meant 'tonight.' I decided to take that as a compliment.

Better than believing the Larnagian was simply horny. "You don't need to use the door, I understand."

"Nope. I just, um, see you here." Wani pointed to her heavy-browed head. "And I go."

"I'm glad you did."

"Mmm, me too." She raised herself on one elbow. "But it is dangerous to keep turning off the sensors. Someone will figure it out, won't they?"

She sounded uncertain. I had no doubt, myself. "If I knew where they were, couldn't I cover them somehow? Then the recording would just be of a dark, silent room." Even were Wani not there, some privacy could be nice.

"Oh, that is very smart, Dave! I'll show you." She jumped up at once. "All in one place." The girl — I had to think of her as a girl, alien or no — pointed them out. Pretty obvious, now that I knew.

"I wonder what it would take to muffle the sound sensors. Maybe I can steal some tape in the lab."

"I'll bring it!" Wani disappeared. Was she going to suddenly appear, nude no less, in Nok and Squid's lab? She hadn't thought that through at all.

Maybe no one would be in there at this hour. And it was unlikely they recorded an empty lab. Still, her act seemed impulsive and risky. Then she was back, with a roll of adhesive in her hand. "I could have taken you with me," she murmured, slipping back under the sheet. "Would you like that, Dave?"

"How about to your own room? I would think no one is watching or recording you."

Wani grimaced. "Messy. But you're right. It would be safer. Okay." She wrapped her hairy arms around me and an instant later I was — elsewhere.

"Whew, too many trips," she said. "Wears me out!"

"I'd rather wear you out in a different way."

"Huh? What's that mean?"

I was beginning to realize Wani was a bit dense. "Like this," I said. She caught on pretty quickly then.

It can't be denied I was pretty worn out myself by the time I showed up in the lab the next day. I hoped Wani had remembered to turn the sensors back on. Easy enough for her to do; I realized that now that I had learned how she could move around.

Our pal MacSquid escorted all three of us humans to the lab the next day. No Tol in sight and a bin of granola bars for our breakfast. Squid and Nok were in a hurry to get to work. On the women, that is. I wasn't of much interest anymore, so I sat and chewed while Nok fussed with one device and then another. I recognized the second one.

"Then it isn't universal," muttered Nok, as the pair of them went over the readings.

"But common, maybe."

"Maybe. At any rate, it probably originated here. *They* originated here."

"So it seems," said Squid. "And that pretty much wraps it up, unless we go down to the planet and take some more measurements. Either way, our findings need to be secured until we get home."

Even I could tell they were pretty excited. Maybe they would break out the booze. Instead, Squid said, "We have clothing for you," pointing them out with one of his tentacles. Coveralls. One size only, which we were not, and all sort of a taupe color.

We looked them over. I don't think any of us were very interested. "Aren't you going to try them on?" asked Nok.

"We need some privacy," I informed them.

The two gave each other those looks again. Maybe thinking 'just like a Larnagian.'

"Dave does anyway," said Donna. "Doesn't matter that much to me." From her look, I do not think Mickie agreed.

"It is not at all important." Squid turned its eye-stalks — all three of them — my direction. "There was a problem with the sensors in your room again last night."

"There are sensors?" I asked.

It whistled, but not very loudly. "Dave is a comedian," it informed Mickie and Donna.

"It's a common condition on Earth," Donna told it. Mickie gave an all-too-knowing nod. She was living with one herself.

"How about in the rest of the universe?" I asked. Had I diverted its interest from the sensors?

"Humor goes hand-in-hand with intelligence," said Nok. "But what were you saying about the sensors?"

"They've gone off-line in Dave's quarters two nights in a row. But the problem doesn't seem to originate there."

"You only missed my snoring," I told him.

"Indeed," agreed the Squid. "Our other guests have proven far more interesting."

Mickie once again colored up. Donna only shrugged, saying, "We tried to give a good show." Maybe she did.

And maybe I should lend Mickie my roll of tape.

"Now, on to other experiments," said Nok. "We have obtained several specimens of this beer you mentioned."

# Chapter 8

"OUR LARNAGIAN IS sick," announced Squid, "and it is certain she caught something from one of you. The captain wants to send you all back immediately."

"I didn't think there had been much contact between you. Outside of Wani's visit to the lab when you were here, Dave."

Yeah, right, Nok. That must have been it. "Will she be alright?" I asked.

"We think so. It is what you refer to as the common cold. Though she seemed hot, not cold."

Donna had looked puzzled through this exchange. "Mickie was at the tail end of a cold. But I thought you said we were unlikely to share infectious diseases."

"So we did," admitted Squid, "and it remains true for you and us. But you and Wani — well, we did suspect that might prove different."

"But we couldn't say anything about it. Still can't."

I had wondered why Wani hadn't shown last night. Not that I couldn't use the rest. Maybe I had carried some of Mickie's germs on me or something like that.

"So, Captain Squid is gonna send us home?" asked Donna.

"It seems likely."

"Though we shall recommend otherwise," added Nok.

I felt let down. I really had been looking forward to seeing another world. I'm pretty sure the women felt the same.

"We'd better do it soon, then," spoke Donna. "We probably aren't even missed yet."

"You could just say you got lost in the woods," I told her.

Mickie practically cackled. "The Great Woodswoman would never admit to such a thing."

Donna smiled at that herself. There was probably truth to it.

"We'll get your vehicle ready, if it is needed," promised Squid. "Or should we smash it so it looks like you had an accident?"

"I can't afford to smash anything I own." I would have lost a lot by not showing up at my gigs. And it might make it difficult to book more.

"Oh, of course. We can compensate you for your time here. Do you prefer gold or this paper stuff?" Nok went to one of the lockers and pulled out a couple thick stacks of bound bills. One each of fifties and hundreds.

"Paper is fine," I told him. "Not that I would turn down gold."

"We would have jettisoned most of it anyway," he said. "No point in carrying it back with us."

"Um, Nok, just how did you get all that?" asked Mickie. "I mean, is it stolen?"

"Stolen? I suppose so. But wasn't it being thrown out?" he asked Squid.

"It was supposed to be. Wani got it for us, of course. We always leave some behind when we gather samples."

"Then it can't be traced to a bank robbery or the like," said Donna. "We're safe, Mick."

"But what about the gold?" persisted her partner. "I know they don't throw that away!"

"No, it was natural gold. From the ground — um, where is it, anyway?" Nok systematically went down the line of lockers.

"Mostly in the geology lab," Squid told him.

"That explains why we only have a few nuggets left," said Nok, holding out a box with more than a few. It must have been pretty heavy; he was using all four arms.

I reached in. "I'll take one as a souvenir." Both women followed my example. Then we got to the banknotes. "Split it three ways?" I asked.

"You've been here longer," objected Mickie. "You should take half." That surprised me some. I think it surprised Donna too but she agreed at once.

"Let's see how much there is first," I said. It took a while to count to eight-hundred thousand. Give or take a few thousand.

"There's too much to fit into our backpacks," Donna pointed out.

Wani must have made more than one trip or maybe she didn't have to carry it personally. I had no idea. Dang, I was forgetting about Wani. Was she going to be okay? I'd even gotten a little fond of her, maybe.

Ah, but I was unlikely to ever see the Larnagian again. There was no way they would let me get close to her on this ship.

"It would be wrong to let them just discard it," I told her. "Take as much as you think you can carry and the rest can be stuffed in my van. Right?" I asked Squid and Nok.

"It can," Squid assured me.

"And I'll let you have as much of it as you want when we get back. If you're willing to go to Alabama for it."

"Or you can bring it to Minneapolis," replied Donna. "But okay." She looked up at the two aliens. We had been kneeling on the floor as we counted. "Assuming we are given the boot here."

"I hope not," stated Nok. "But it does seem likely."

Squid agreed. "So it does. We do have time to investigate some more booze."

"Our farewell party," murmured Mickie.

"Be sure to send a sample to Wani," I said. "Our apology to her. The bourbon."

"That's always a good cold medicine," added Donna.

Our alien friends were introduced to rum that evening. Nok rather liked the *anejo*.

"We'll send some of this to our Larnagian too," he vowed. "I am told she is quite miserable."

"That she is," agreed Squid. "I act as doctor on this vessel, officially, but hardly ever am called on to do anything of that sort. Probably I should be with her right now." It sipped some more white rum. I don't think it had quite made up its mind about the stuff.

"I'm a nurse," offered Donna. "I could look at her if you wish."

"Nah, the Cap would have my tentacles if I let you near her. Wani seems to have a great deal of, um, liquid discharge in her nasal passages."

"A runny nose. That's normal. Is her throat sore?"

"It is. That's normal too?"

"Yep. And then a cough to finish things off and she'll be all over it. Give her fluids," advised Donna, "and give it a week or so."

If her immune system could handle an alien disease at all. I was sure Donna was aware of this — and that there was absolutely nothing we could do about it.

"I hope that's so. The female acts like she thinks she's dying."

"She'll figure out she isn't, sooner or later."

Squid whistled. "Maybe! Larnagians are not that bright, on the whole."

Really? Then Wani was typical?

"Their unique gift got them out among the worlds before their race was ready," said Nok.

"Exactly. Most of their technology was borrowed from here and there."

"But," Nok pointed out, "none of us would be here were it otherwise." He drained his rum. "Nothing to do now but see what tomorrow brings."

As always, Nok. As always.

# Chapter 9

AS SOON AS I turned out the lighting in my room — I could command that vocally now — I felt my way to the sensors and thoroughly covered them with tape. I didn't expect a sick Wani to show up but the expected isn't always what happens.

The night was a restless one. I don't think I slept much anyway and had peeled the adhesive away and dressed well before anyone came for me. It was Squid.

"The captain won't change its mind. We're to send you down as soon as possible." It rolled down the hallway, opposite the direction of the lab. "I'm going to inform the females. The sensors show they are awake."

"Do you need Wani for this?" I asked. "Transporting us?"

"There are shuttles. That's how we've done most of our research. Your radar doesn't see them at all. But your eyes can, so we mostly work at night. That's fairly soon in your longitude." It paused. It might have been the women's door but all of them looked the same, gray metal set in gray metal walls. "Easier to drop you and your vehicle first, probably. The place from which we took you?"

"Might as well put me down at my own house. It's out in the country and no one will see." I didn't even keep animals. I tended to be on the road too much to take care of them properly.

"Alright." It looked down at the device it held. "They are, as your race puts it, decent." The door slid open.

"We're going home," I announced. "Grab your gear."

They seemed to have anticipated this. Hiking boots were on feet, backpacks full of loot were ready to shoulder. I handed each of them one of my business cards. Yes, I carried cards and even did business.

"Cullman, Alabama?" read Mickie. "Where's that?"

"North end of the state. Convenient to Nashville." Which was one reason I chose the area, along with the low cost of property. "I'm not in the town. Out in the country a good way."

"Gimme another card," requested Donna. She scribbled on the back of it with a stub of pencil from her pocket, and handed it back. 'Donna Johanson,' it said, with a Minneapolis address. Under that she had added 'Michelle Vogel.' No phone number. That was okay with me.

We would get in touch when we got in touch. And if we didn't, I had their money. "This way," said Squid. Another squid-star had joined it. Mac, I was pretty certain. We'd never gone this direction before, opposite the way to the labs. Where did Wani bunk? I'd only been there when she transported me. Down an elevator, along another hallway, this one wider.

I knew they called this a small ship but it seemed pretty big to me. Even more so when we emerged into a sort of hangar. There were a couple flying saucers in it. I don't know what else to call them.

"There you are," called Nok. "We just stowed your — what do you call it, Dave?"

"Van?"

"Van. Right. With the currency inside. I hope it's enough."

I think I would like doing business with these people. No, those who followed would have more sense about such things. If more followed. Wani's illness could scare them off, couldn't it? We might be quarantined or something.

"We're going to go down with you," said Squid. "We feel responsible."

"And well you should," Donna told it. "You'd best set us down near the edge of the forest. Near Deer River. That's where my car is."

"We'll figure out where that is," said a Sormog I didn't know. Maybe the pilot. Female. Yes, larger than Nok again. That must be normal. "Get aboard and we'll get you home."

There was nothing to see but walls inside the saucer. And my van, lashed down on the deck. "Those flight couches will probably work for you," continued the Sormog, waving a couple of her arms in their direction. She gave us a looking over. "You'd fit nicely into a Larnagian couch, wouldn't you? Only one of those."

"You take it, Mickie," I said. "We'll fit better in these big ones." Meant for Sormogs, I figured. There were little bucket shaped seats, too. Squid settled into one of those. Mac had disappeared. Probably not coming down with us. A couple minutes later I asked, "When are we leaving?"

"Already on our way," answered Squid. "Let me get the screen working." It fiddled with its hand-held device — tentacle-held device, I should say. Space and stars appeared on a screen in front of us. "A different camera — yes." A big ungainly lump blotted out most of the stars in this one.

"That's the ship?" I hadn't seen it from outside before.

"It is. Let me get the other direction." Earth. There it was and growing rather quickly. I couldn't feel a thing to indicate we were traveling. That changed a couple minutes later.

"This is why we have couches," commented Nok, as the craft started shaking and bouncing. "If we went in more slowly it would be smoother."

"But we want to get you home quickly," Squid said.

"Ah, starting to settle down." The Gulf of Mexico was looming on the screen. I think all three of we humans gasped as we dove toward it. But of course the saucer leveled off and sped northward. Again, there wasn't much to feel. Despite the time spent on that big ship, nothing impressed me so much as this ride. It drove home how advanced these visitors were.

"Alabama coming up," came a voice. "Past Birmingham, right? That's it below us."

"Right," I squawked out.

"It's nice your planet is advanced enough to provide satellite positioning. This would be guesswork, otherwise."

I had to laugh. These aliens were using GPS to find my house. I had never used it myself. The van was too old to have it and I avoided my cell phone as much as possible. Cell coverage was kind of minimal at my place. That was the excuse I gave, anyway, for my Luddite ways.

That night I slept in my own bed. After unpacking all that money from the van, naturally. I assumed the women had been dropped back into the wilderness.

I told everyone that I had been sick and spent the last month in a hospital bed. I was vague about which hospital. Maybe some believed it. As far as I could tell, no one had come out into the sticks to check on me.

And my van ran even better than when it was new. That had been a long time ago.

I canceled any scheduled gigs. Still recovering, I let folks know. I needed some time to figure things out and count my money. Our money. Some of it should be Mickie and Donna's. Mickie had been quick to contact me through my website. Yes, yes, I do have one of those, and internet on a satellite connection. That's all that's available this far from everything.

That's unimportant and uninteresting. The two of them were safe at home, they would get in touch, and so on. Things settled down. I even wrote some songs. I'd get back to touring in time, even if I didn't need to make any money.

Two weeks passed, three, a month. Space was feeling more like a dream each day. Had Nok and Squid even been real? Well, the money was real so I guess they were too. I was settling down with a book one evening, in the big blue recliner I kept in what I called my studio. I should get busy and record again, I told myself. My attention wandered from the page and to the unused equipment. I could afford to take the time now.

A sudden thump behind me. "Dave!"

I knew that voice. She probably couldn't even see me, enveloped in this chair. I looked around to see Wani, her eyes darting here and there.

"Oh, there you are!" The Larnagian girl was at my side before I could get myself sitting up straight.

"Why are you here?" I asked. "Is everything alright?"

"Everything is terrible," she sobbed, "and everything is wonderful. I am pregnant!"

# PART II. ON THE ROAD

## Chapter 10

SHE COULDN'T MEAN I was the father, could she? That was impossible. We were different species from different worlds.

"How long?" I asked.

"A month. You could have guessed that, Dave! I wouldn't have known but the doctor told me. The one you called Squid." Wani giggled. "We were both surprised!"

"But — how?"

She cocked her head at me. "You know how babies are made!"

By now I was on my feet and directing her toward the kitchen. "Yes, yes. I guess I meant who, not how."

Wani looked puzzled. "There wasn't anyone else on the ship."

"Didn't Doctor Squid tell you that isn't possible?"

"No. It whistled quite a long time after I told it about us. Then it made me promise not to tell anyone else."

I should fix something to eat. What might poison a Larnagian? I'd have to be careful. "I'll fix some tea," I told her. That should be safe enough.

"No bourbon?" asked Wani.

"Bad for the baby." At least I knew that much. I'd have to worry about poisoning it too. I motioned her to a chair and put the kettle on. "So Squid, um —" I wasn't at all sure how to put this. "It thinks I could be the father?"

She nodded solemnly. It and Nok *had* tested my genetics and a bunch of other things they didn't explain. The women's too. They should know, shouldn't they? And they had gone out of their way to keep it secret.

The whistle of the kettle brought me out of my reverie. I think it actually startled Wani. Maybe they didn't make tea on whatever far-flung world she came from. I poured the hot water over a couple bags and got ice from the freezer while they steeped.

"I hope you like tea." That sounded extraordinarily lame, Dave. Sweet? Lemon? I didn't know and she wouldn't know. We would have to experiment. As I filled two tall glasses with ice, I asked, "How did our Doctor Squid happen to discover your, um, condition?"

"It gave me a physical after I was sick. You caused that too, didn't you?"

"It would seem likely." And neither one at all intentional.

"All you do is get me in trouble!" She giggled at her joke. "It wanted to be sure I was well enough to get the ship back home."

Made sense. I found lemon juice. Bottled, I had no fresh lemons on hand. Sugar. An iced tea spoon for Wani. I don't like sweet tea myself, despite being southern. Then I decided not to risk fruit juice right then and put the lemon back. "I've no idea whether you will like this," I told her, "but it's likely to be safe. We'll have to try some other things out later. So I guess you did get the ship home?"

"Yep. And as soon as it was safe I jumped right back here to you."

All that distance — not that I knew how far it was — and without a ship. "Will someone come looking for you?"

Wani shrugged. "They won't know where I went."

Squid and Nok would guess. I could guess nothing, not when they had kept so much secret.

"Well, here's our first experiment in Alabama food," I said, pouring the hot tea over the ice. Wani seemed delighted by the

44

crackling it made. "I like it just like this but some put sweetener in their tea." I didn't know a word for sugar in Alienese. Should I try to teach her English? I wasn't about to introduce her around.

She sipped her drink and reached for the sugar bowl. "Hmm." Wani wet a finger and dipped it in, licked it off. "We have this at home." She shoveled several spoonfuls into her tea, stirred, and drank deeply. "Much better."

Straight sugar, as straight alcohol, was perhaps safe for most aliens. I did begin to suspect my young guest could eat anything I could. Best to be cautious, though.

"You look tired," I told her.

"I am. It's a long jump. And I just jumped the other direction yesterday."

"You, um, show the ship the way or something like that?"

She yawned. "Something like that. I just go and they follow. I —" Another yawn. "Don't understand that part. Computers or somethin'" She lay her head down on her crossed arms.

"We'd better get you into a bed."

"Mmm, that's what got me into trouble, Dave."

I didn't know whether caffeine didn't effect her or she was too worn out for it to matter but Wani was snoring in seconds. She wasn't large, a hundred pounds maybe or a hundred and five. I scooped her up and put her in my own bed, pulled the blanket up. It can get cool overnight in the hills.

Then I went and emailed Mickie Vogel. Just maybe she and Donna should know about this.

# Chapter 11

"DID YOU HEAR about the Bigfoot sighting?" asked Joe.

"Around here?"

"In town. Big hairy guy. They say he just appeared outa nowhere and then vanished again."

Most of the time, I would simply nod and forget something like this. This time I nodded and didn't forget. "Maybe he meant to go to Birmingham and got lost." I slipped my credit card out of the reader, grabbed my bags. It had taken some time to pick out things Wani might be able to eat and there wasn't that much selection at this local convenience store.

I think Joe sold more beer and snacks to fishermen than anything else. No beer for my guest. Definitely not milk. No way would Wani be able to digest it. I'd given her cream of rice this morning and that seemed to go down alright.

My turn was ahead, a dirt road, and then another turn, onto another dirt road and up a hill. Not that there weren't plenty of ups and downs before I got there. It looked like Wani had stayed inside like I asked her. In fact, I found her asleep again, curled up in my recliner this time. Either she hadn't bothered to put the leg rest up or couldn't figure out how.

What was I going to do with her? She couldn't stay in my house the rest of her life and if she went out — well, there would be more Bigfoot sightings. Littlefoot. That would be more accurate. She stirred as I was putting away the groceries.

"Oh, more food. I'm very hungry, Dave."

I wasn't surprised. Could I try her on eggs? But first — "I think one of your people was spotted in the area. A Larnagian."

"Oh-oh." That was all she had to offer, so I went on.

"The reports said he was big but I don't know whether to believe them." Or any of it. I wouldn't have a few weeks ago.

"You think he was looking for me?"

"It would seem like a good guess. And a good guess that you were here. Wouldn't he be able to, um, see you in his head and come here?"

She laughed at my ignorance. "Not unless he already knows where I am. It's just blind jumping if he doesn't."

Ah. "But he has learned where my neighborhood is. Or she."

"Might be Daddy," she said. "Don't wanna go home!"

And I didn't want this Larnagian finding us. He might be just a bit pissed. That 'secret' Nok and Squid were keeping was in the back of my mind too. Best no aliens knew where we were.

"Here," I said, tossing her a bag of hard candy. I figured that was safe. "I think we're going on the road, Wani."

"On which road?"

"The road to Minnesota." I had decided that just that second, but it made sense. "I need to pack some food and clothes in the van." And all the money.

"Mmm-mmm. Okay. Mmm." She had already filled her mouth with the sweets.

First, I should inform Donna and Mickie we were headed their way. I was carrying their cash so they should have no reason to object. Just email them quickly and then — what was that in the news feed? 'Bigfoot Spotted in Cullman Alabama.' Someone had snapped a phone pic. Yeah, that looked like a Larnagian. But *big*. Maybe the photo made it look larger than it was. He was.

It was a good idea to get out of its vicinity anyway. Brief email dispatched, I turned to packing the van. On a whim, pretty much, I put in my usual music equipment, just as if I were traveling to a gig. All the food in the house. I would have to buy more, of course, but I'd rather not stop any sooner than needed. Clothes — what could Wani wear? All she had brought with her was the one coverall.

I'm not so big. She probably would be okay in some of my stuff. If Wani had a hat pulled low over her eyes, folks might not even notice her. At a distance. The brow ridges were her most obvious difference.

"Wani," I asked, when I finished, "you can't, ah, see the girls we're going to visit, can you?" Maybe we could leap there without the van.

"Huh-uh, Dave. I looked in the records and found your house. From when they left you here. That's why I was able to come to you."

"Then so could other Larnagians? I mean, if they had access to the records?"

"Maybe. But I know you better. Makes it easier to see you." She had a rather self-satisfied smile.

They wouldn't be able to locate us on the road, anyway. The sooner we left, the better. "Let's go." I bundled her into the van and got out of there, not the way I had come in but north toward Huntsville on the back roads. I could catch the Interstate further up.

Did I glimpse the form of a large, manlike figure standing on the hilltop as I sped away, leaving red dust in my wake? Maybe it was my imagination. I saw nothing more but hills and cars, driving on until I reached Nashville.

Wani got carsick long before then. It could have been the food, it could have been the pregnancy. More likely, just riding was to blame. It seemed to be a new experience for her. We'd both been having a lot of those lately.

It was evening when I pulled into Music City. Should I get a motel? It might be smarter to keep driving, pull over for a couple hours at a rest area further up. Darn, I wasn't even sure of the best route to Minneapolis from there. I filled up the tank though I was getting exceptionally good mileage. Thanks to Gof and whatever he did to my engine!

I checked my map before taking off again. I-24. I should get on I-24. On through the night I drove, while Wani slept in the back. On toward a city I'd never seen, toward people I barely knew, for reasons I didn't understand.

Pretty much like any other gig.

# Chapter 12

"IT'S COLD HERE," complained Wani.

Fall in Minnesota. Yeah, it was cold. "We may not stay very long." Where was the apartment? It should be on the left. There. I entered the parking lot. All open design here, townhouses in groups of four, no halls to get Wani through. That was good. Unit Twenty-eight. I pulled into a space right at its front door. Maybe one of the our hosts had thought to leave it open for us.

"Wrap up." The Larnagian pulled a blanket around her. "Head too. Keep your ears warm." And her face hidden.

"Okay, Dave." She understood why I asked. Wani didn't have to be a genius for that. "I've only seen them on screens."

She had said this before. "And they haven't seen you at all," I reminded her. "Don't worry, they'll behave."

The door cracked open before we reached it, a narrow pathway of light spilling onto the sidewalk. "Come on in," called Donna. She had the presence of mind to use Alienese.

What would these two think of Wani? In a sense, Nok and Squid were less disturbing. They were simply alien, with nothing human about them. The Larnagian was both familiar and strange, human and alien.

At first. I barely noticed she was different anymore. "This is Wani," I announced, as she let the blanket fall from around her head and onto her shoulders.

"Welcome to our home, Wani," said Miss Vogel. "I'm Mickie and that is Donna." She indicated her partner with a jerk of her head. Donna seemed uncertain about this visitor. Maybe surprised and nothing more, though I had warned them. Thoroughly warned them.

"Yes, welcome. Come on in. Um, you eat, um, Dave, she eats regular food, right?"

"So far she has devoured anything I've handed to her." Wani giggled at that. It was true. She had an appetite and nothing seemed to have bothered her after that initial carsickness. "But no dairy."

"Not even yogurt? She might be able to handle that."

Maybe she could. Donna was a nurse so she should be more knowledgeable about it. "Yogurt? Dave wouldn't buy me frozen yogurt. And then he ate his own right in front of me!"

"That's a guy for you," commented Mickie. "And some women. Oh, whoever picked out those clothes for you?"

"Hey, they're good clothes," I objected. "I've worn 'em myself on occasion." I gave the apartment a looking over. Living and dining, straight through. Kitchen probably behind those stairs. I'd seen more than a few pretty much like it. Furnishings rather mismatched. Two personalities at work, but not working together.

"They'd probably fit me better," said Donna. "But let's worry about that later and get some food into you." She gave me a wink. "Then we can count the money."

"Do I get some of it?" asked Wani. She turned to me. "Or will you just buy me things?"

I could only shake my head. "Whatever you want, Wani."

"Dave will need to pay you child support," piped up Mickie.

"Of course. We will have many children and he will support them all!" This was the first I'd heard of it. "How many children live here? You have lots of room!"

It was Donna who managed to get out an answer, clearly fighting an urge to break into laughter. "No children, Wani."

"None? You must not have very good men! Or do you share one?" When there was no immediate answer, she plowed on. "No matter. I'll lend you Dave. I'm hungry!"

"That's kind of you," Donna told her. "Hmm, I was going to

order pizza but Dave's probably right about the dairy thing. Though hard cheese might be okay."

"Not the time to experiment," I said.

"You're right. Does she handle gluten okay?".

"She's been gobbling pretzels without any problem."

"And donuts! I love donuts!"

We ended up with spaghetti. A sated and exhausted Wani ended up in a spare bedroom upstairs that looked more like a home office. We sat around the table and finished off the bottle of red that should have gone with the pasta. It was best not to break it out with Wani there.

"Even though you were able to get her pregnant," said Donna, "there might be complications with the child. It might not survive to birth."

I hadn't really had time to think about that. I knew just enough about that sort of thing to realize it could be true. "I — hope not." That was true wasn't it? "For Wani's sake, mostly."

"Wani might be better off back on her own world," Mickie put in.

"I know. I also know there is a lot more going on than just Wani and me. That's why I ran with her."

"And about all you can do is wait and see what happens."

"That's true about most of life, Donna," I told her.

"Yep," agreed Mickie. "Any vino left?" I refilled for her.

"Wani isn't, well, very bright, is she?" asked Donna. "Will that bother you? I mean, if you stay together?" Her tone suggested she thought this unlikely.

I sipped the merlot before answering. "One thing I've come to recognize as I grow older and supposedly wiser is that prejudice against the less intelligent is still prejudice. Who the person is matters far more than how smart they are."

"Well said," stated Mickie, raising her glass to me. "But the question then is, who the hell *is* Wani?"

"Your guess is as good as mine."

# Chapter 13

"WE CAN'T HOLE up in your apartment indefinitely," I said.

Donna considered this. "You probably could. There's certainly room for the four of us."

"Five, eventually," Mickie pointed out.

"Someone with medical training should be around to deliver the baby — and here I am."

Donna was volunteering? That was surprisingly good of her. But — "There is no way we are staying in Minnesota through the winter."

Mickie snickered. "I usually feel that way around this time of year."

"Then let's get out. We have money enough to go where we want. I'll give notice today." Donna looked at her watch. "I'd better get to my shift. Do we do it?"

"But my job at the magazine —"

"Which will never pay enough to live on. You can write your novel or something."

Mickie didn't take all that long to consider it. "Yeah! Let's do it. I'll turn in my resignation today too."

"Good enough. We'll figure out a plan of action later on. I'm off," said Donna, and swept out the door.

"I suspect it will take a couple weeks to get everything worked out," felt Mickie. "You and Wani will stay here till then, right?"

"I suppose." I did feel a little leery of staying in one place that long. "We'll talk about it tonight. Do you have to get to work?"

"Nah, not till ten. Donna has an early shift at the clinic. More coffee?"

"Sure. I think I'll go check on Wani first, though."

She filled my cup. "I'll do it." She was headed to the stairs before I was out of my chair, so I let her.

The four of us on a road trip? Not at all what I had in mind when I headed here. Not that I really had anything in mind. Just getting away from my place. I went into the living room and switched on the television. The morning news —

"Bigfoot sighted in Chippewa National Forest," the announcer was saying. "More after the break."

Oh, hell. A minute later, the girls came down, Wani wrapped in a pink bath robe. Mickie's undoubtedly. "There is a Larnagian here in Minnesota looking for us," I reported. "We should hit the road again."

"How?" asked Mickie. "Could he follow you?"

"He must know where you and Donna were deposited." Hmm, so he wouldn't have any idea where to look in Minneapolis. Still, there was no point in tempting fate. "We'll head out as soon as we can." That would be best, wouldn't it? And safest for our hosts. "If you and Donna still want, you can follow later. I'll let you know where we are."

"Can we eat first?" asked Wani. "Running on an empty stomach is no fun."

We were all out the door by Nine, Mickie on her way to catch a bus, Wani and I getting everything stowed in the van. I had left half the money. No qualms about that now, as I figured we were splitting it four ways with Wani in the picture. Hey, maybe Wani could get us more. Only if we needed it though.

I'd told Mickie I thought we would head east. It seemed as good a direction as any. I'd call or they'd call and we'd see how things went. I didn't really expect to see them again, and hoped Donna hadn't quit her job. But then, they had four-hundred thousand dollars now so maybe it didn't matter much.

"On the road again," I sang as we pulled out.

"What are you doing, Dave?" Wani looked quite puzzled.

"Driving. Or did you mean the, um —" I didn't know a word for singing in Alienese.

"The funny noise you were making. I liked it."

"That's good because it's what I do for a living. Doesn't your race have music?" Did any aliens? Oh, they must or there wouldn't be a word in Alienese.

"Of course we do, silly, but it doesn't sound anything like that! Was that your own language?"

"Uh-huh. I should teach you English, probably. There are only three humans in this whole world you can talk to." I chuckled. "Too bad the radio is broken or we could have been listening all the way from Alabama. In English."

"That's the radio?" She reached forward and turned a knob. Music filled the van, much clearer than I had ever heard it before.

"Well I'll be. Gof must have fixed it too."

We were halfway through Wisconsin when an unmistakable voice broke in. "Dave? Are you there?"

"Squid?" Could it hear me?

Apparently so. "We've been trying to get to you for days," it said. "Is Wani with you?"

"She is."

"Ah. We suspected that was where she went. Are you alright, Wani?"

"Yes, Doctor. I'm on a road trip!"

"That's good. All in all, it might have been the best move. But I must impress on you, young lady, do not let any of your people know where you are or that you are pregnant. It would raise too many questions that should not be answered now."

She nodded, which is not the best answer on a radio. "I think a Larnagian has been looking for us," I told him.

"Someone let Wani's father see the logs from your shuttle. He knows nothing, not even whether she is on Earth. He's just following any leads he can and one led to you."

"To Donna and Mickie too."

Wani sniffled. "I don't want Daddy to be sad."

"The lives of millions and millions of people on Earth are at risk," warned Squid. "Please do not contact him."

That got her attention. "Dave too? Would someone hurt Dave?"

"Dave too."

"Then I'll be quiet," she promised.

"We're going to head south," I said. "I'm thinking Florida perhaps."

"We'll stay in touch. And we have a tracker in your vehicle so we know where you are. Just Nok and me; no one else knows anything about it."

"You came back, I assume? In orbit?"

"We did. We had to bring along a navigator, of course. That's a danger we couldn't avoid. Now I'll return you to your regularly scheduled program." Squid's whistle was cut off by a Willie Nelson tune.

"Why would my people want to hurt you?" wondered Wani. She had sat and thought for a few minutes before asking this.

"I really don't know, Wani," I answered. "I think it might be because we are, well, related in some way. How we could be, I can't begin to figure out. But you and I couldn't be having a child if we weren't."

"And that's why it is a secret. Okay, Dave. Do we have to sleep in the van again tonight?"

"Ah, one night in a bed spoiled you!" I teased. I'd slept on the floor myself. The couch I'd been offered felt too confining.

"You'll have to spoil me a lot soon."

"And I shall," I promised.

# Chapter 14

MY PHONE BUZZED. I'd been keeping it turned on since we left Minnesota.

"Dave Ladd Productions," I answered.

"Do you always say that?" laughed Donna.

"Force of habit. I've been doing it for years. Are you two alright?"

"We are. No more Bigfoot sightings in the area. It was looking for Wani, wasn't it?"

"It was. He was. It's her dad."

"Oh, maybe there's a ray-gun marriage in the future!"

"Would that were our only worry. So, what are your plans?"

"We both quit our jobs. We'll follow you as soon as we tie things up here. A couple weeks. And I know you're going to say we don't need to get involved, so just save it Mister Ladd."

"I don't have to tell you where I am." I was halfway serious about that.

"And who would look after that girl? You?"

She had a point. "I'm pointing toward the east coast right now," I said. "Maybe the Carolinas. Then we could head on to Florida for the winter." Just when would the baby arrive anyway? If Wani took a human nine months then around the beginning of May? That seemed right.

"It's gonna be hard to keep Wani covered up in Florida," she warned.

"I'll have to find a place in the country." Like my own house. Too bad I couldn't go back there. I couldn't even have the mail forwarded, though I had stopped it before leaving and all my bills were supposed to be paid automatically. You learn to set that sort of thing up when you're on the road a lot.

"We should pick a place to meet before then."

"Yeah. I'm in Illinois now. Reckon I'll be making that big left turn soon. Lemme find my map — oh, did I wake you, Wani? Wani says hi. Um, the map. Don't wanta drive through Indianapolis. Maybe I'll get off the Interstates for a while."

"Is there any reason to hurry?" Donna asked.

"I do want to cross the Appalachians before there is snow. I'm not big on driving in the snow."

"No wonder you got out of Minnesota. So you'll head for like North Carolina?"

"I think so. It shouldn't take long, no matter what roads I choose."

"Yeah. So call when you get settled in a spot."

"Right." I wondered if I should have mentioned Squid after we ended the call.

Nine PM. No sense in parking here any longer. "Well, Wani, I think it's time I start driving again."

"Teach me how," came her sleepy response.

"When we find a place to stay for a while," I promised. I might break that promise. I headed south.

Wani slept through the river crossings, the Wabash, the Ohio. Dawn came in Kentucky. I was tired.

"I'm the one who needs to sleep a while now," I told her.

"I'll drive," she offered. I had hoped she'd forgotten that idea.

Too bad she couldn't teleport us and the van across the mountains. "We're not that far from Nashville now," I said.

"Music City. Near your home. Are you going home, Dave?"

"No. I don't know whether it would be safe or not, but I'm not going to take a chance." I had friends in Nashville. Probably not a good idea to contact them, either. Better to turn east and head toward Knoxville or Chattanooga. We could stay there overnight and cross the mountains tomorrow.

60

So I slogged on. It was early afternoon when we pulled into Knoxville. "What do you say to a motel room tonight, Wani? This isn't any place to sleep in the van." It was kind of cold, too.

"Alright with me. I have to hide, right?"

"Some," I admitted. "Pull your hat down and we should be safe." I picked a decent looking motel a bit outside of town, nestled below a wooded hill. Not many cars. I remarked on that in the office.

"Peak season for autumn leaves is past," the lady at the desk told me. "Tourism drops way off now."

I nodded and checked us in as Dave and Juanita Ladd. She might have eyed me a tad suspiciously when I paid cash. People just don't do that so much anymore.

No problem getting Wani into the room. Not many eyes to see her and she was well covered. Our drinks were all warm by this time. For that matter we were getting low on food. I should stock up when I reached Asheville in the morning. In the meantime —

"I'll get us something to drink from a machine," I told her. "Be right back."

"Okay, Dave." She was entranced by the television, flipping through the channels, even if she didn't understand a single word. I wondered if she realized it wasn't real.

There were a couple of middle-aged guys in camouflage coveralls and beards at the machines. I gave a polite nod and got bottles of iced tea.

One of the men squinted at me for a moment. "Hey, you're that country singer!"

"So I am," I responded. I was not not overjoyed to be recognized. Not now. Another time, maybe.

"Dave Ladd," said his buddy.

The first guy looked doubtful. "Isn't he dead?"

"Only my career." I gave the pair a looking over. "Isn't it early for hunting season?"

"Bow-hunting," said one. "We get first crack." He looked at the bottles in my hand. "We have plenty of beer if you'd like to stop by. Room Eight."

"Okay. Gotta get these back to, um, my roadie."

"Bring him too."

As long as I was fabricating a story I might as well go all the way. "Can't let him near the stuff, y'know?" I confided. They thought they did know and nodded wisely. I got back to our room as quickly as I could.

Wani had given up on the tee-vee. 'Wheel of Fortune' was on. I turned it off. "Will you sing more for me, Dave?" she suddenly asked.

Why not? "After we eat." I could bring a guitar in from the van and run through my handful of almost-hits. It would be a change.

I could have gone right to sleep when we finished, but I had promised, hadn't I? I went out and got my knock-around acoustic, an old Ovation. I couldn't begin to tell you how many road trips we had shared.

Someone called. "Hey, Dave, give us a song." The guys from earlier. They had been at the beer they had mentioned, that was for sure. I could smell it. I've had a lifetime of smelling beer.

"Yeah." The one plopped down in a weathered cedar chair by my door. The other stood there, a little unsteadily. It might be simplest just to give them what they wanted and send them on their way.

"Um, let's not do it in the room." No way I wanted them in there with Wani. I settled into one of the chairs, ran my thumb over the strings. Close enough to being in tune. Would these guys even remember my songs? I could probably give them anything.

I began finger-picking the opening to one. My hands were stiff from gripping a steering wheel and there was some buzzing. Not that my technique is so great even when I'm not tired. The door opened beside me and Wani stuck her head out. She hadn't bothered to pull her hat low and she looked, well, like a Larna-gian. These guys were just too close to her not to see it. They stared at her.

"Man, that's one ugly nigger," said one.

The other stepped back. "That ain't no dude," he said. "That's a gow-rilla!" He pulled out a hunting knife. "Get back, Dave. I'll take care of this!" The man stumbled more-or-less forward. His confused and equally inebriated buddy stumbled the opposite direction.

Wani disappeared.

# Chapter 15

IT WAS NOT hard to convince the police that two drunken rednecks had seen things that weren't there. "Maybe it was a bear," mumbled one of the pair.

"No," insisted the other, "it was a gow-rilla. A big one!"

"Or maybe it was Bigfoot," I commented, with a wink to the officer.

"Yeah, Bigfoot! That's it!" In the end, both were shepherded back to their room to sleep it off.

"We get a lot of this sort of thing this time of year," one of the policemen had confided. "Worse when gun season starts. Then they might have shot their imaginary Bigfoot."

I could only be thankful they hadn't been carrying firearms. Or their bows, for that matter. But now — where had Wani gone? I sat maybe an hour with the motel room door hanging open — despite the cold — watching for her to pop back somewhere. In the room, in the van. I had no idea. For all I knew, she might have been scared enough to jump back home to her daddy's protection.

My phone buzzed. Donna's number. "Hello?"

"Are you missing a girl, Dave?"

"Wani's with you?"

"She is. She said it was the first place she could think of when she was startled. What happened, anyway?"

I explained it all. "Ah. Wani's definitely shaken up but okay, I think. She also says she's not entirely sure she could teleport back to you. A little mixed up about where you are or —" She lowered her voice a tad. "A little afraid. Don't know which. Maybe both."

"I don't blame her. I'll drive back and pick her up."

"No, no, Dave, don't bother. We'll be on our way in a few days and we can just bring her along. You go find a place for us to stay."

That did seem like a reasonable plan. "Good enough," I

agreed. "I'm headed to Asheville in the morning and then in the general direction of the Atlantic. I'll let you know where I end up. Thanks for looking after Wani and, um, don't let her eat too much junk food." I had been guilty of that myself but it's hard to avoid on the road.

"I am a health professional!" she declared. "Trust me." Though she laughed then, I did trust her. She and Mickie didn't have to get involved in this at all. I was grateful.

I was gone before dawn and watched the sun rise over the Appalachian peaks ahead of me. I kind of wished Wani had been there to see it. Did they have mountains where she came from? I had no idea what her home was like. I'd have to ask.

For that matter, what sort of worlds spawned Squid-stars and Sormogs? It was stupid of me not to be more curious. But then, I was expecting to go see some of those worlds first hand. It could still happen, Dave, I told myself. Not that this world wasn't awe-inspiring enough on a morning like this, with the mist-hidden valleys below, the mountains bathed in the golden glow of morning. But yeah, the leaves were past their peak, weren't they?

Ha. That was hardly important! Down I-40 into North Carolina, through Asheville and on toward the sun. Toward Wilmington, I had decided. I liked the town, had considered moving there once. Maybe I wouldn't get all the way there but it gave me a destination. I wouldn't get there today. I mean, in theory I certainly could but I did not intend to hurry. I'd keep my eye open for a place to stay a while. Maybe a campground.

Yes, camping. That's what I should do. I stopped in Statesville and bought a roomy and rather expensive tent. Hey, I could afford it now. I exited the Interstate there too, and angled southeasterly on less traveled roads. That night I spent in a state park. It only took me an hour or so to figure out how to pitch the tent. Then I finally did get the guitar out and played some. It had been too long.

Onward the next morning, across the Pee Dee, past Fort Bragg. Nothing caught my eye. Maybe I *would* end up in Wilmington. Winter rentals could be cheap, not that I wanted to stay through winter.

Lumberton. Now it looked promising and it was on the Interstate. I could hit the road south quickly. There were a couple state parks between it and Wilmington but they might shut down their campsites in the winter. If they had campsites. I spent the night in a noisy motel there. By the end of the next day, cash had rented me a trailer outside town for a month. I called Minneapolis.

Or I called Donna. I didn't have a number for Mickie, though she was my email contact. "That's great," she said. "We'll be on the road in about a week. Depends on how quickly we get everything tied up here. Stuff to put in storage and all that, y'know?"

Plus they had probably given two weeks notice at their jobs. Maybe that didn't matter at Mickie's job. That seemed kind of casual. "Yeah, I know. How's Wani holding up?"

"Well enough. No morning sickness yet but it's likely to come. As long as it's not while we're on the road!"

"I hope she's not going stir-crazy in your place. Tell her 'hi' for me. When you head this way I'll give you more exact directions."

"Just the address will do fine. I'm modern. I have GPS."

"Oh, right." One car, I assumed. Donna's. I didn't think Mickie had a vehicle. "So, within a couple weeks. I guess I'll see you then."

What I would do with myself the next two weeks, I had no idea. Maybe I would drive down to Wilmington anyway, just for the heck of it. Hey, maybe I could even play there. I'd have to check it out.

I stepped out into the weed-filled yard. The moon was rising behind bare branches. A faint humming, barely noticeable, came from somewhere. An insect? It seemed too cold for that.

A flying saucer slowly descended next to my truck. Maybe it wouldn't be so boring here after all.

# Chapter 16.

"SO WANI IS no longer with you?"

"Temporarily. We'll all be back together soon." I do not think Nok approved. Too bad.

"We could go get her," he said to Squid.

"To what purpose? She's as safe there as anywhere." It turned it eye-stalks to me. "Maybe it's time we explained some things."

I thought so too. "You're smart, Dave," it continued. "We underestimated you at first, when we discovered your race is related to the Larnagians. You know they are, um, not so intelligent."

"So I understand. What I do not understand is how we could be related."

Nok answered. "*That* we understood at once, when we tested your genetics. It was always known the Larnagians did not originate on their home planet."

"But no one knew where. The Larnagians, included," said Squid.

The Sormog picked it up again. "Here's the generally accepted theory. Two or three hundred thousand years ago, the ancestors of all Larnagians jumped into space from somewhere and landed on the planet they now call home. A pair of them, most likely. Now we know they jumped from here."

"Most likely," added Squid.

"So — they are primitive humans. Erectus or heidelbergensis or something like that."

"Or sapiens, since you can apparently interbreed."

Apparently. "Then what exactly is the problem?"

"Humans can teleport too. Some of them. If the Larnagians were made aware of this they might well all leap here at once and try to kill you. They would not like the idea of competition."

Wait. Humans could jump to other planets? "Some of us, you say?"

"It is far from universal but fairly common. Maybe as many as one in ten, but we don't have a big enough sample to be precise," said Squid.

Nok added, "It *is* universal among Larnagians."

"In humans it seems to correlate with what might be termed an artistic temperament. You have the ability, Dave. So does Mickie. We could read it in both of you."

"Then why haven't I ever teleported? Why doesn't anyone?"

"Probably humans do it unwittingly from time to time, and have been for hundreds of thousands of years. Millions, even. People do disappear without explanation at times, do they not?"

"Yeah." I was nowhere near convinced.

"There must have been many failures before a couple of Larnagians found a planet where they could survive. Many failures since, too. Landings on poisonous worlds, on airless worlds, perhaps just in empty space. And most of those jumps would have been single individuals who would leave no offspring even if they did survive."

"Then I can teleport?" I asked.

"In theory," Nok answered. "The Larnagians have training methods. They've been developing their techniques a very long time."

I would have to ask Wani about this. "If enough of us learned them, we would be less vulnerable to an attack."

"This has been discussed. A great deal has been discussed since we secretly presented our findings. Representatives of over a hundred worlds are trying to come up with a solution. The thing is, we could not stop the Larnagians if they did attack you. We can not travel between the stars without them."

69

"Or without *you*, perhaps," said Squid. "If you humans learn to teleport."

"You understand that we are not just interested in saving lives on Earth, though that is certainly important enough on its own. There is also the fact that the Larnagian monopoly on interstellar travel would finally be broken. There would be a second race to compete with them. Everyone is excited by this idea. The problem will be protecting you until you are ready to take your place."

Ah. So economics played its role, as always. "They will learn, sooner or later," I pointed out.

"Indeed so. Let us hope our leaders figure something out."

"It has been suggested transporting some numbers of you to other planets," said Nok. "As a precaution. But the Larnagians would undoubtedly be curious about the reason for it."

"Or conversely," Squid said, "sending guards here to protect you. But that would arouse suspicions as well."

"Are the Larnagians all that dangerous?" I asked. "I mean, if they were they would have conquered the universe by now."

"If they were brainier they just might have," admitted Nok. "The other worlds have learned how to deal with them. Your people haven't."

"And the adult males can be rather, ah, belligerent. As well as rather large. There is a marked sexual dimorphism."

"Another reason most navigators are young females."

"So Wani and I can't do much but hide and see how things turn out, huh?" And these guys — and their superiors — would be interested in our child. I wasn't sure I trusted them much more than the Larnagians. "Well then, let's turn our attention to other matters. I have a bottle of brandy ready for your analysis."

"Ah, yes," said Squid. "We mustn't neglect science."

# Chapter 17

TEN DAYS LATER a Volvo station wagon pulled up in front of the trailer. I hadn't done much in the interval. Did drive over to Wilmington but it was kind of dead there and a cold breeze blew off the ocean. It would be good to get out of here. It would be good to get somewhere warmer.

No need to pay another month of rent on this shabby mobile home, either. An eager Wani sprinted to the house. I was glad to see her too. I'll admit it.

I stood there, my arm around Wani, and watched the women crawl from the vehicle. "That doesn't look very comfortable for sleeping," I remarked.

"Yet we did," said Mickie. "We took turns driving and stopped only for restroom breaks."

"Damn, I'm stiff," Donna said. "It's good to finally be here."

Not for long. "Come on in. I have lots to tell you." And I did. They sat around the peeling Formica-topped table, eating and listening. I saw no reason not to let Wani know the whole story too.

"Well," said Donna, and nothing more for a while. She gave her partner a long look. "Then Mickie could jump to other places just like Wani?"

"In theory." I asked Wani, "Do you understand all this?"

"Yes, Dave. You are all — Larnagians. Just like me." She giggled. "But not as pretty." Then she got serious. "The doctor is right. My people might want to hurt you."

Wani got it quite well. I shouldn't underestimate her.

"He said we could learn to jump. He said there were training methods."

"Oh! I could teach you! Both of you."

Mickie looked like she had mixed feelings about this. I know

I did. "Our survival might depend on it," I said, directing it at no one in particular but intending it for Mickie. Maybe human survival did. There was no way of knowing that and no point in thinking that far ahead. Learn what we could do, first.

"And mine, if I'm with you," noted Donna. "When does training camp start?"

I shrugged. "I'd say that's up to our instructor. But I really would like to get out of this place." Not right this minute. They looked bushed. "When you are rested up a little."

"And off to Florida?" asked Mickie. "Is that still what you have in mind?"

"It seems like a good destination. Only a day away, too." I shouldn't be forcing anything on them. "But I'm not in charge."

Wani snickered. "Sure, Dave."

Donna laughed outright at that. "We are going to entrust ourselves to your patriarchal leadership, Mister Ladd. Don't disappoint us!"

So be it. "Rest well then and we'll set off for our promised land in the morning. I'm ready to get out of this place."

"A caravan south," said Mickie. "Next stop, Miami Beach?"

I definitely had no intentions of going that far. "I'm thinking a campground or house further north. In fact, there are several state parks we could aim toward for tomorrow night."

"We have a tent," announced Donna.

"So do I."

Both were in use the next night, way down upon the Suwanee River. It had been an uneventful trip, on the Interstate at first and then increasingly narrower highways into the town of White Springs. I knew White Springs and the park there. I'd performed at the annual folk festival held in it. That was the sort of thing has-been country singers were inclined to do.

Needless to say, no one at the park recognized me. "We can stay for two weeks tops," I told my companions, "and then move on to another campground. Or find a place to rent, maybe."

"It's not a good idea for Wani to be in a public campground," stated Donna. "You know that."

Yeah, I knew that. "I have a friend in the Tampa area who owns land up here." A former girlfriend but they needn't know that. "I could call her up and ask if we could camp on it." That had been in the back of my mind for some time. I'd hoped to keep it there.

"I like it here," said Wani. "I wish I could move around more."

Okay, I would do it. Shoot, I could probably just squat there without asking. I knew the way. I talked to Susan that night and got the go-ahead from her. Give it a day or two first, I told myself. Enjoy some of the amenities of the park campground. It would be primitive on Susan's property.

But Wani wouldn't need to hide. She sat with us around our campfire that evening, well bundled up, a cap pulled low on her forehead. The weather was cool, so the heavy clothing was necessary anyway. Northern Florida can get surprisingly chilly — surprising to Yankees.

"Does it get cold where you come from, Wani?" asked Mickie.

"Where I grew up, yeah." She was attempting to toast a marshmallow without great success, and that took most of her attention. It slipped off her stick and into the flames. "The Larnagian home planet is pretty hot. I've visited."

So they didn't all live on one planet. That was probably good to know. Being Larnagians and able to teleport, it would be pretty difficult to keep them in one place, wouldn't it?

"My family home is on the next planet out," she continued.

"Hmm, like the next one out from this planet. The red one. What do you call it?"

"Mars."

"Mars. Okay. Ganc is like Mars. My people have always jumped back and forth between the two. But it wasn't always good to live there!"

I could imagine. Once they 'borrowed' technology, as my alien friends put it, from other worlds things would have changed.

"Would you like to go to Mars?" she suddenly asked. "I could take you!"

"We couldn't breath, could we?" wondered Donna. "And it would be bitterly cold, I would think."

"Wouldn't matter. We'd only look for a few seconds and come back."

That sounded far too risky to me. I'm sure Donna shared my feelings. "I'm game," declared Mickie. "When can we try it?"

"Right now." Wani took her hand and both disappeared. I didn't even have time to say 'damn' before Mickie popped back, followed by Wani, a couple seconds later. The reappearances were so close to each other one might almost have missed the difference in time.

Wani looked at the trembling Earth woman. "You jumped back on your own!"

"D-d-did I?"

"I think you did," I said. Squid and Nok had said she should have the ability. Me, too. I didn't really believe them.

"You must have clicked your heels together three times," said Donna.

"I just knew I wanted to come back. It was so dark and cold and — and strange."

"That seemed rather reckless, Wani," I said. I could have used stronger words but I was certainly not going to scold her.

"Impetuous," said Donna.

Mickie laughed and added, "Impulsive."

Wani grinned. "Irresponsible! My teachers would say I don't always think things through."

I wondered if that were a trait of Larnagians in general. I'd probably find out one of these days. "Speaking of teachers," I said, "I think Mickie needs one. Me too, maybe."

Wani frowned. "How would I bring one here?"

"He means you," Donna said, her voice soft and with the slightest hint of amusement.

"Oh, right! I said I would." But she didn't seem so enthusiastic about the idea now. Second thoughts, maybe. Almost apologetically, she told us, "I'm not sure I know how. Teachers first work for many years as navigators. This was only my second trip."

It was very much a guess but I said, "You must be pretty good or they wouldn't have given you the job."

That brightened her up. Flattery can have that effect — not on old cynical types like me, perhaps, but Wani was willing to eat it up. "That is so, Dave!"

"Then teach us," spoke Mickie. "I'd like to know how I did that."

Wani gave us a knowing smile. "You've had your first lesson. Dave too. Just by jumping with me. It opens you up to your gift." She giggled. "That's the way my teacher put it."

So maybe I could teleport? I looked at Donna, sitting across the fire pit from me and decided to go visit her. A moment later I was standing halfway in the fire. "Daaaamn!" I jumped out as quickly as I could. Good thing I was wearing shoes.

Wani turned to Mickie. "Some students are more talented than others," she observed.

# Chapter 18

"YOU'VE BECOME FOND of Wani, haven't you? Beyond whatever duty you might have felt toward her and, um, your child." Donna and I stood on a low bluff, looking out over the Suwanee. The sun was rising and our companions were still in their sleeping bags. There had been a light frost overnight, painting the open ground white.

"No point in denying it," I replied. "But it's not, well, love. Not in the romantic sense."

She only smiled at this. "No, I don't think Wani is your soul mate." A silence for a few moments. "That doesn't mean you don't make good mates anyway. Better'n me and Mickie maybe."

I had seen better couples. I'd seen worse, too. "Is her new ability going to change things, you think?"

"Undoubtedly. Let's get back and pack up."

By early afternoon, I had found Susan's ten acres, back a winding dirt road. It was somewhat low-lying land and parts of it surely flooded from time to time. That was unlikely to be a problem at this time of year.

There was no house on the property. A small shed stood on a cleared patch of higher ground, and there was a rock-lined fire pit. "I'm not going to want to drive the wagon in and out that road too often," said Donna.

"There won't be much reason to," I replied, "but I reckon we'll go stir-crazy if we don't get out now and again." An occasional grocery trip to White Springs or Lake City, at least.

"Donna would," said Mickie. "I can go a long time without seeing people and be completely happy."

Me too. "Let's get the tents up."

Mickie looked around and suddenly realized something. "There's no electric? I'll need to charge my laptop." She had been pecking away at it regularly. Maybe writing that novel Donna had mentioned.

"We'll go into town and buy a generator," I decided. "Some kerosene lanterns, too, and — damn, there's a lot of stuff we're going to need, isn't there?" If we were going to live primitive, I intended to do it in comfort.

"Axes," said Wani. "For firewood."

"Definitely," agreed Donna. "You and I can go gather fallen limbs right now, while these two set up camp."

Wani did tend to get in the way when we were pitching the tents. Shoot, I tended to get in my own way. Mickie and I had my larger one erected by the time they came back with arms full of branches. "There's room enough for all of us in this one," observed Donna, dumping her firewood.

Mickie immediately shot her a dark look. There could be any number of reasons for that. Wani seemed oblivious to their tension. I hadn't seen much of that sort of thing in the Larnagian girl, but she was human, after all. Thoroughly human I had come to realize.

"We'd better allow for some privacy," I said. It didn't matter that much to me. It didn't seem to matter to Donna. Our companions were of a different temperament. Living with these three through the winter might be more challenging than I had envisioned.

And Wani's pregnancy would be advancing. I couldn't forget that. We should be long gone before she gave birth. I certainly hoped that was so. Where to? Maybe it would be safe to go back to my place by then. Maybe it was safe now.

The next day, however, I needed to go shopping for all those items we had thought of. Donna was the obvious companion for this. She knew more about camping and roughing it in general than any of us. Lake City was the place to shop. We could fill up the van with all we needed.

We found our way to pavement and headed south. "Are you going to be alright with hanging out in the woods all winter?" I asked. "Or maybe I should ask if Mickie will be."

"Mickie will do fine. She's been writing lots. Obsessively, if you will." She chuckled at that. "If she stops, there might be trouble. And I'll be able to hike around and keep myself entertained, at least for a while. How 'bout you, Dave?"

A good question. *Too* good a question. "I'll be the one to get restless first. I know that." The story of my life. "I won't run off, of course, but I might get cranky."

"I just hope that Mickie and I can keep it together. If we can't, one of us might run off."

"Troubles?"

"Yeah. Every couple has them, right?"

"In my experience, yeah. Which is why I'm single." Wait. "Well, I guess I'm not actually single now, am I?"

"We'll have to ask Wani."

No, we wouldn't. I hadn't the slightest doubt the Larnagian considered us a couple. Mates. Whatever. "Have you two been together long?"

"A couple years." Donna sighed. "I guess Mickie always knew she was a lesbian. I took longer to choose a side." I'd never seen why anyone needed to 'choose a side.' I would not, however, comment on that.

Instead, I smiled and asked, "She convinced you?"

"She did. But she knows I am still attracted to guys. Physically attracted."

"Which is not the same as falling in love," I said.

"Exactly." We rode on in silence for a couple minutes, entering the outskirts of the town.

"You don't think my presence will be a problem, do you?" I finally asked.

She only laughed. "I think I can resist you, Dave!"

I laughed too. It had been kind of an absurd question. "Wani did offer to share me with you two."

"I wonder if that's part of her culture. Polygamy."

"I don't know," I replied, "but we'll have all winter to learn about her."

"And her to learn about us. She's doing a good job of picking up English." That had started while Wani stayed with them in Minneapolis.

We bought everything we could think of. More than we needed, no doubt. Toilet paper. Drinking water. Shovels to dig a latrine. We finished off by filling several cans with gas for the shiny new generator and headed the laden van back north.

Dusk was filling the woods with shadow as we crept along the dirt road into our camp. Donna suddenly seemed attentive to something, leaning toward the open window. She liked fresh air.

"Do you hear that?" she asked. "It sounds like music. Sort of."

I brought the van to a halt and cranked down my own window. "Banjo," I said. "That often sounds sort of like music." I had an immediate suspicion as to its origin. "We may have a visitor." The van moved forward again, slowly. I needed the headlights now.

Next to Donna's Volvo sat a pickup truck. A fire burned by our pair of tents and a figure sat by that fire, playing the banjo. Playing it quite well, I'll admit.

"You know that guy?" asked Donna, as I rolled to a halt.

"Not a guy," I replied. "That's Susan. My ex."

# PART III. OUT THERE

## Chapter 19

"YOU WERE MARRIED, Dave?" She sounded slightly incredulous.

I would have been too. "Fortunately, no. Ex-girlfriend. Long-term."

She snickered. "Oh, an XLTGF!"

"And her dog." I could see Doo lolling at Susan's side. I wondered what Wani had made of him. Did Larnagians keep pets?

Well, they certainly saw a lot of strange lifeforms as they roamed the stars. I guess a dog wouldn't bother her. Maybe she would bother the dog — Wani might be a new and different scent to Doo. Ha, what if he caught a whiff of Nok or Squid?

Nothing to do but make the best of this, get out and say hello. Susan spoke before I could. "Quite a harem you have here, Dave."

I ignored that. "This is Donna Johanson," I said. "Susan Rossi. I assume you've introduced yourself to the others, Susan."

"That she has," said Mickie, "and told us tales of you. You have an interesting past, Dave."

Susan gave me a look that was somewhere between sardonic and affectionate. I was never sure with her. "Not as interesting as his present. I got to read Mick's ongoing account."

Doo meandered over and sniffed at me. Satisfied, he moved on to Donna. She knelt and scratched behind his ears. I was not at all surprised she was a dog person.

Wani had remained silent, sitting and watching the rest of us. Did she feel left out in some way? I wouldn't blame her, not one bit. "Let's unpack all this stuff," I said. "Did you bring a tent, Susan?"

"You mean I can't share yours?" she replied, with arch innocence.

That peeved me more than a little. If we weren't guests on her property, I might have said something I shouldn't. I answered, as dryly as I could manage, "No." Nothing more. I could see Wani smile at that.

Susan did have a tent. Small, but that was her choice, wasn't it? We helped her get it up, and then got all the stuff Donna and I had purchased out of the van and made a start at setting up a more comfortable camp. But it was late and dark and getting nippy. "We can get back to this in the morning," said Donna. We were all in agreement.

At least we had lanterns now. That was a definite improvement. When we cranked the generator tomorrow we could even have electric lights, if we wished. Probably best not to run it that much, I told myself, though I wasn't sure why we shouldn't.

"Susan's music is funny sounding," remarked Wani as we settled down in our own roomy tent, "but I like it. I like her. Is she your mate?"

"She was, once. No more." I smiled into the darkness. "We were both too cranky to get along."

"You're not cranky, Dave," she assured me, snuggling closer. I could have said she didn't know me well enough yet. Fortunately, I had the sense to hold my tongue. I don't always.

"Dave?" she whispered.

"Yes, Wani?"

"Do you only like me because I'm pregnant? I'm not smart like — like all the other females here. I know it."

My first impulse was to disagree with her. "Why would you think that, Wani? You're plenty smart."

She sighed. "Larnagians aren't smart. We know this. The

82

other races out there —" I think she waved an arm in the direction of the unseen sky. "Make jokes about us. But they need us." There was a bit of vehemence in this last statement.

"And I need you," I told her. That time, I managed to be smart. "Just you and who you are."

I was not sure how true it was. But I did like her. Dang, I liked her better than any of those three women sleeping in the other tents. I had to make sure she never felt intimidated by them. Never felt inferior.

She had fallen asleep but I couldn't for a while. I could only wonder about where we would go next. Something would happen, eventually, and that was kind of my fault. Wani's too, when it came down to it. If we hadn't had sex, if she hadn't gotten pregnant, the secret of Earth could have been remained a secret indefinitely. Could we find a place to hide? Maybe on one of that multitude of worlds out there.

But none would support human life. Oh, some might but we were unlikely to find them. We couldn't survive unless we depended on others. Hospitality might become captivity. A breeding program even. I could think of all sorts of unwelcome scenarios. Ah, but we could always leap away. As could any Larnagian. Any attempt at that sort of thing by aliens would be sure to fail.

We were already an experiment. Of that I had no doubt. They were watching to see if Wani's pregnancy successfully came to term. Squid might have suggested an abortion otherwise; that would have prevented all that followed. He might even have performed one without her knowledge. I had no idea what sort of beliefs or feelings any of them had about such an action.

I most definitely would not suggest it. The light of a hunters' moon filtered into our tent. I could make out the Larnagian girl's

83

form beneath the blankets, soundly sleeping. In time, I joined her in slumber.

# Chapter 20

"SUSAN CAN'T JUMP," declared Wani. "She's like Donna."

I didn't know how she could be sure but I was willing to take her word. Nok could wave an instrument in her direction some-time, perhaps, and corroborate it. In the mean time, Mickie and I were being given lessons.

That largely consisted of practice and learning to get a firm picture of our destination in our heads. It was easier if there was an individual we knew at the other end of our jump. There was never any problem with coming back to camp, however erratic the outward teleport might be.

Susan hung around. She claimed she simply was taking a little vacation and might have come up here anyway. "I do intend to build a cabin someday," she said. "Make this my home base."

She had been saying that years ago, too. We had even talked about living together here. I reckon her interest might have waned after the breakup.

"No upcoming gigs?" I asked her.

"Only lessons. I canceled all of those for a while." She had students. I knew that. I haven't the patience to teach, myself.

But Wani did. She proved surprisingly good at it. "You are very old to be beginners," she told us. "Most Larnagians learn to jump when they are little kids."

"How little?" wondered Mickie. "Toddlers?"

"Oh, no. They might get in trouble. Mothers never teleport with their children until they are six or so, so they don't pick up the ability too early."

Mothers? How about fathers? I wondered if Mickie was thinking the same thing but neither of us voiced it. "But you have special teachers, right?" I asked.

"Yep. Especially those of us who are going to be navigators."

We continued to learn over the next couple weeks. Only a very few long jumps were made, in the company of Wani, sometimes one of us choosing our destination, sometimes our instructor. She always made us handle the leap back.

"We could jump up to the ship," said Wani. "I could or you could, Dave. We both know it well enough. Maybe Mickie too."

Visit Squid and Nok? "But how do we know its location? Isn't it moving?" I assumed it was in orbit.

"You have to learn to *see* it. Then you will know where it is." She had said this with mock seriousness. Then she giggled. "But you are right, it's hard when it doesn't stay in one place. Hey, Doo, would you like to go meet aliens?"

The dog seemed agreeable to the idea. He seemed agreeable to anything Wani said. The two had hit it off from the start.

"Doesn't she consider herself an alien?" whispered Mickie. I could answer that only with a shrug. Maybe Wani did see herself as one of us. Genetically, she *was* one of us.

What I did say was, "I should turn on the van's radio more often. One of them might try to contact us."

I decided to do that later, sitting in the van, listening. I could pick up a country station but I wasn't too fond of where country music had gone. Just as it wasn't too fond of me. There was classical from Gainesville that came and went.

Susan climbed in and took the front passenger seat. She didn't know about Nok and Squid speaking to me this way. She probably just thought I was getting away from things for a few minutes.

"It's about time I skedaddled back home," she said. "You know you're welcome to stay here as long as you want. As long as you need."

"Thanks. It might be best for us to stay put through winter."

Susan nodded. "And then where? This is no place for Wani to give birth."

"Maybe back to my place." It could be safe. It might be now.

"What after that? You can't hide the girl forever. That's Mozart, isn't it?"

"Hayden. I'm hoping my friends upstairs have a plan by then." Because I sure didn't.

"And you intend to stay with Wani? That doesn't seem very workable, Dave. You're too different."

"And you and I were too alike," I shot back. Which was true but was also a bit of being defensive on my part.

"Maybe so. Anyway, her appearance will be a problem. The face mostly but she's kind of hairy too." Susan snickered. "Not that she's much homelier than me."

Which was true, not that I would acknowledge it. Wani did have a bit more hair than average, to be sure, on her forearms, her legs, and a thick bush in her crotch. "I've seen hairier women," I said. I could have said some were Italian but Susan probably would have hit me. I have grown older and wiser since we were together. "But, yeah, her face is hard to hide."

"Just what is she? Like a Neanderthal or something? You did say her ancestors came from Earth."

"She doesn't look much like a Neanderthal. From further back maybe. And of course evolved some since, just like we did." She only nodded in response, so I went on. "No way we could know. They keep finding more early humans scattered all over the place."

"Like those Deni-something-or-others," she said.

"Yeah. It's all just guessing." With their access to her race's genetics, the aliens orbiting above might be able to give an answer. "One thing I recognize now is that Wani isn't stupid." To me, she seemed pretty close to average human intelligence. Probably ninety-something if given an IQ test.

"No, she isn't. Not terribly bright either." That too I had to agree with. "She needs to be around people like herself. Wani can't be a recluse like you, Dave."

"I agree. And right now there's not a damn thing I can do about it."

# Chapter 21

"I WAS LISTENING in while you spoke with your friend," Squid informed me. The alien's saucer had set down in the dirt entry road, as that was the widest open space available. It had still managed to knock down some small trees on each side.

"Eavesdropping? Not very good manners," felt Mickie.

Susan didn't have an opinion. She was still taken aback by the aliens' appearance, warn her though I had. This little space craft we were sitting in might seem a bit astonishing — if not intimidating — as well. The only other occupant was a Sormogian pilot, a female. Possibly the one that had brought us back to the planet a few months ago. She paid us little attention.

Wani and Donna were off cutting firewood. I wondered if Nok and Squid had known this and thought it a good time to visit. I also wondered when they had learned to speak English, for that was what they were using, probably for Susan's sake. If their machine could teach us Alienese I guess it could teach them English.

It would be handy for listening in on Earth too, wouldn't it? Wani had been picking up English pretty well, and more so since Susan arrived. The two had gabbed quite a bit and I was rarely called on to translate anymore.

"So, you have learned to teleport? Both of you?" asked Nok.

"We're learning," I admitted.

"Your offspring will certainly have the ability, in that Wani and you do," said Squid. "We have isolated the primary gene involved."

"Recessive, of course," Nok added.

"So it might not be a good idea for Wani to jump as her pregnancy advances. It could have unforeseen effects on the child."

"She is aware of this. All Larnagians are. That is one reason young female Larnagians are given solo duty on ships. It keeps them out of trouble."

"They *are* a horny bunch. As you discovered. I've even heard of them propositioning Sormogs."

That wasn't very flattering to me. Susan was smirking.

Nok took up the narrative. "It can be noted that those who are chosen to be navigators are, um, more intelligent than average. The cream of the Larnagian population, really."

"So Wani is an extra-smart Larnadoon?" asked Susan.

"She is. Wani is from a distinguished family too. Her father is a leader of their people."

"The ones on Ganc?" I hazarded.

"Indeed," said Squid. "I didn't know you were aware of Ganc."

Mickie's voice came soft, almost as a sigh. "Wani speaks of it sometimes. I think she is homesick."

Wani wasn't the only one. Mickie might well be the most content of us all, writing away here in the middle of nowhere. But she sensed how the rest of us felt.

"There aren't so many of them on Ganc, are there?" I asked.

"Not near as many as on Larnag. There are a couple other isolated colonies on planets barely suited to sustaining life. It is difficult for any race to find such a place but Larnagians do have an advantage there."

"Yes," agreed Nok. "They can search more quickly than we who need ships, but our ships are an advantage in themselves." He paused for a few seconds before continuing on a slightly different tack. "It may be the first to jump to Larnag remembered the way back to Earth. There might have been a certain amount of teleporting back and forth for a few generations, possibly even carrying mates to their new home."

"Only two individuals would have been a very small gene

pool," Squid pointed out. "Maybe even an untenable one for their survival."

That particular waving of the antennae I knew to be Nok's version of a nod. "It's even possible they took plants and animals. That needs further investigation. Be that as it may, the location of their original home was eventually forgotten."

"They wouldn't have needed it once they were established, would they?" I asked.

Susan took that up. "Probably more interested in living their lives and propagating their species. Especially if they are as 'horny' as you claim."

"No hornier than we are," said Mickie. "It's a human thing, don't you think?"

"Absolutely," said Susan and I almost simultaneously.

"Considering how many there are of you, I can believe it," remarked Squid. It turned its eye stalks to its companion. "Maybe we should let the Larnagians murder them all." It didn't whistle but I knew it wanted to. "Do we really want to unleash smarter, hornier Larnagians on the universe?"

"It's too late," said Nok. "They've already learned to teleport. Hmm, you say this one can't?" He looked through a box at his side and pulled out a small device. He pointed it at Susan. "No, doesn't have the genes. Doesn't have the *gene*, I should say." He showed the reading to Squid.

"Only one copy of it. Your offspring might have the ability," Squid informed her. Its attention turned to me. "Have you two mated?"

I hesitated. That's not surprising. Susan jumped in. "Many times."

"But no, um, offspring," I added.

"Too bad. You should mate with the other one," declared Squid.

Mickie sputtered. I thought for a moment she had felt offended but realized she was trying not to laugh. "For the sake of science?" she asked.

"You would?" asked Nok, apparently quite serious. "I thought you were homosexual."

"She jokes with you, Nok," Squid told him. "As I joked with her."

"Hey guys, you in there?" came a voice.

"Yeah, Donna," Mickie called back. "Come on in."

Wani came through the doorway first. She was starting to show, that was for sure. Still a long time though and it hadn't prevented her from sprinting up the ramp. Donna followed at a more leisurely pace.

"We were just discussing whether I should jump Dave," Mickie informed her. "For the advancement of the human race, you know?"

"And then we'd all go live on a distant planet and raise a mess of talented kids," contributed Susan.

"Oh, can we?" asked Wani.

Damn, she'd taken it seriously. Donna decided to as well. "Maybe it's not as ridiculous an idea as it sounds."

Maybe it wasn't. Maybe a little human colony somewhere was a prudent idea. I was absolutely certain those alien leaders out there had considered it. But it would only keep a few of us safe. What of the rest of humanity? Curmudgeon and misanthrope though I could be, that was something that concerned me.

"As a last resort maybe?" I said.

I think perhaps we all agreed with that, Nok and Squid included.

"It is to be hoped a better solution can be found," said Nok. "It may end up with this planet being quarantined for a while."

"Which could mean centuries," interjected Squid.

"Possibly. Hide its existence. But you would have to leave. All of you."

"Even me?" asked Susan. "I wasn't part of this!"

"You know too much of it," felt Nok.

Squid was not so sure of that. "She can't teleport so it may not matter. But we can not have people jumping into the universe from this planet. It would give its existence away, sooner or later."

"Then you could stay too, Donna," said Mickie. There was no inflection to her voice to tell me exactly how she felt about it.

"And in the mean time there would be an attempt to find a solution," I said.

"We might be the solution," Mickie pointed out. "If we're off breeding on some other world."

"But we'd be just as likely to reveal its existence if we started teleporting. Or our descendants did."

"It doesn't look good any way, does it?" asked Susan.

"So we need a real solution, and soon," I stated.

"Agreed," said Squid. "Meanwhile, it might be wise not to teleport much."

Nok said, "If any."

"It would be best for your child, Wani. You know that, right? Only if you have no choice."

She nodded. "Right, Doctor Squid. But the others can practice, can't they?"

"Only little jumps. Definitely not to other worlds."

That seemed reasonable. "Are you guys going to hang around?" I asked our alien friends. "I think we should have a party before Susan takes off. We'll even let her play her banjo."

"It sounds very beautiful!" enthused Wani.

"Well, I suppose we could. How about it, Pot?" This was addressed to their pilot. Apparently she had been taught English too.

"Alright with me. Captain said to use my discretion."

"You're invited too," I told her.

We were all heading out the door and down the ramp when a woman's voice came from behind us, in Alienese this time. "Where are you all going?" A young Larnagian stood there, a girl. Surely the navigator from the space ship somewhere above us.

"This changes things," observed Squid.

"Muca!" yelled Wani, and ran to embrace her.

# Chapter 22

"WE WENT TO school together," Wani explained. "Come on and join the party, Muca. Oh, this is Doo."

Muca shrank back a little as the dog nuzzled her hand but was soon petting him. Donna and I threw more wood onto the fire and we all settled down around it. There was plenty of beer.

Muca gave her friend a long look. "Who is the father?"

"It's a secret," Wani replied. That was sensible of her.

The Larnagian girl didn't press her on it. "We've been worried about you," she said. "Especially your dad."

"Please don't tell anyone! I have a reason for hiding out."

Muca shrugged her shoulders and guzzled some of the beer. I think Wani envied the fact that her friend could drink and she wasn't allowed.

A little later she whispered to me, "If I thought she might tattle, I'd put a knife in her."

I was taken aback by the statement, to be sure. "I thought she was your friend."

"But you're my man. That's more important."

So Wani really did consider me husband or mate or whatever the position might be in Larnagian culture. This was not going to end with us simply parting, going back to our very different lives. Not that our old lives existed anymore. No, not for either of us.

Muca looked no more like Wani than Donna looked like Mickie or Mickie looked like Susan. To an alien eye that might all seem much the same but I was used to Wani now. I knew her. The newcomer was a little stockier. She wore the same jumpsuit Wani had on board the space ship so it was hard to tell much else about her body. The face was broader, making her brow ridges seem a little less pronounced.

I wondered if she came from Ganc too. Not for long. It was

supposed to be a party, a farewell to Susan. That was what should have my attention. We played some tunes together, just like in the old days. Of course, Susan could play circles around me. I never resented that and still don't.

But the evening inevitably wound down. Squid remarked, "These swamps remind me of home. Much colder though." It sidled a little closer to the fire. Maybe a little too close considering its tendency to dry out. I thought it might be time to get our aliens back to their ship. Where had Nok disappeared to?

Maybe in the saucer. I went up the ramp and there were Pot and Nok, their long caterpillar bodies rearing up, writhing and intertwining and — well, Nok could never accuse humans of being horny again. I backed out and let them get on with getting it on.

Too much beer for them? I had no way of knowing anything about Sormogian mating customs. But I did whisper of my inadvertent discovery to Squid. I figured it might be important for it to know.

Its whistle-laugh was relatively subdued. "It was the cold air. It stimulated Pot's reproductive cycle." So the cold brought her into heat? "And like any male Sormog, he was ready when it happened."

Maybe that was why they kept it so warm up in the ship. Both these species were better off with it that way. That could be one reason they were paired, too, but most likely only one reason.

"They'll be ready to travel in an hour or two," Squid went on. "Of course, Pot will need to lay her eggs when we get back to the ship." Its eye stalks swiveled, scanning the camp. "I say, where did our navigator go?"

It didn't take long to realize she had slipped away. Squid got on his communicator or radio or whatever you would call it and asked the ship if she had returned. She had, and then jumped away again.

"I fear she has gone to turn Wani in," it said.

"She would betray her friend?" asked Donna. The same question was in all our minds but she put it in words first.

"Her loyalty to, um, her tribe? Not sure that's the right word," mused Squid. "Other loyalties, anyway. They may have seemed more important to her."

"Well, I'm getting out of here," declared Susan. "Right now, not in the morning!" Which wasn't that far away.

I thought it was a pretty good idea. "We all should. Let's pack."

By now, Pot and Nok had emerged from the saucer-shuttle, and Squid went over to confer with them. Both Sormogs seemed lethargic. I didn't pay much attention nor care much. Where should we head? Muca could corroborate that Wani was on Earth and give directions to the camp but once we got away no one, alien or otherwise, should be able to find us.

Nok addressed us. "We think you should all come up to the ship."

"No way," Susan replied. "I'm going home. Take them up if you want." She jerked her head in my general direction.

"Really, it should be all," the Sormog persisted. "It would be far safer for everyone concerned."

"I'm sorry," said Squid, messing about with some relatively large piece of equipment they had brought out. It had a handle like a suitcase. I saw Nok give that equivalent of a shrug with his antennae.

Then everything went dark.

# Chapter 23

THIS WAS JUST like the first time the aliens had abducted me — a blackout, an awakening on their ship.

We were all laid out there on thin pallets. Not comfortable at all. Yeah, it was Nok and Squid's lab back on the ship. "Damn," I rasped out, "all our stuff was down there." Not that it actually mattered but I wanted something to complain about.

"And we brought it all up," said Squid. "Every vehicle, every canvas shelter."

"We wanted to leave as little evidence as possible," added Squid.

"So we, um, burnt everything in the area before we left."

"What? You burnt my woods?" Susan had awakened. It didn't dawn on me for a few seconds that she had spoken Alienese. They must have had her in the language lab.

In fact, everyone was starting to stir. Where was Wani? She wasn't with us.

"Only the campsite," Nok assured her. "Now we have to get out of here. I fear we will have to ask Wani to jump despite her pregnancy."

To this Squid added, "She's with the captain now, charting a destination."

"You know we can teleport too," Mickie told him.

"But you do not know any of planets we might travel to."

Maybe not but did that matter. "If you just want to get away from here, either of us could do it. Me and Mickie, I mean."

"This is true," admitted Squid. It activated the intercom and spoke into the air at some length in Squidish, rather than Alienese. My guess was it was talking to the captain of this ship. The answer came in the same language of wheezes, clucks, and chortles.

Less than a minute later the door slid open. "I am to escort humans to the captain," said the squid-star that entered. "I'm not sure which ones."

"We two," Mickie said, taking my arm. "Lead on, MacSquid." It was Mac, wasn't it? Our very own concierge.

We went up the elevator this time. Something scuttled by in the hall as we exited, small and metallic-looking. "What was that, Mac?"

"Robot. Haven't you seen one before? They do much work around the ship."

"First I've heard of it." Mickie had apparently heard nothing, either, or maybe she was ignoring us. She seemed subdued.

"It is true we attended to you ourselves," said Mac. "That is protocol. Here is the captain's office. I shall wait outside."

The captain looked pretty much like the other squids aboard. One of its limbs, or lobes, was only about half normal size. The captain must have mated — or whatever one called squid-star reproduction — sometime recently. I didn't know how quickly they regenerated so I could not even guess how recently.

In fact, if they kept splitting off parts of themselves and regenerating, did they grow old? I might think to put that question to the doctor sometime. Right now my attention turned to Wani, who sat in a comfortable-looking padded chair. One of the few pieces of furniture I had seen here that seemed designed for a Larnagian.

"Oh, Dave," said she, "the captain says you might jump instead of me. Do you think you can?"

"I think I should," stated Mickie.

"Which is better?" asked the captain.

Wani looked us both over. "Mickie," she admitted. "The female."

"Not surprising. Let's go. Take us anywhere as long as it's away from here."

Wani directed Mickie toward the chair. "Put your hands here and here," she said, "and just go. The ship will follow."

"Okay," said Mickie, and teleported.

"A rather timid jump," remarked the captain. "We are only at the next planet out."

"Mars?" I asked. The place she went when she first jumped with Wani. Maybe it was on her mind.

"It wasn't what I intended." She seemed perplexed.

"No problem," Wani assured her. "Rest and try again later."

"Or I could take us somewhere. Unless you think this is safe enough, sir," I said to the captain.

"It does make me nervous to be here," it replied. Something beeped. "What is it?" it asked.

"Ship just appeared by Earth. No, two of them now," came a Sormogian voice.

The captain looked at me. "We got away just in time but we need to go further." It waved a tentacle toward the chair.

Anywhere, huh? I settled myself in, placed my hands as Mickie had, and went.

Wow. I felt dizzy. I tried to stand but couldn't. The teleport had knocked me silly.

"That was stupid," scolded Wani. "It is dangerous to jump so far."

"Which no one ever told me."

The captain whistled. "I think you will survive. Dave, is it not? A long leap to be sure. We're not quite sure where we are."

"Nor am I," I admitted.

"That makes it all the more dangerous," Wani said, shaking

her head. "Just like a male. That's why they don't become naviga-tors!"

It was Mickie who laughed this time. Or snickered. But she made no comment.

"Anyway," said the captain. "We're not going to be detected now. That was a danger where we were. Had a Larnagian known we were there she could have jumped aboard or brought one of the ships."

"Or he," murmured Wani. "There might be males."

"Ah, sent by your father. Yes, that is indeed possible. Can you walk now, Dave? Best you get to quarters and rest while we figure out where you put us." A low whistle, maybe the equivalent of a chuckle, erupted, and it turned to an array of instruments. Wani and Mickie helped me from the room.

"Are there rooms for us?" Mickie asked MacSquid.

"There are," it said and led the way without further word. I'm pretty sure they were the same rooms we had before. Wani stayed with me.

"It's just as big as mine," she decided, "so I might as well. Besides, the other room stinks of Muca." I doubted this was true — though the whole ship smelled a bit ripe to me — but didn't argue it. Wani was certainly welcome to share my bed.

I assumed the others found their own beds. I didn't feel up to checking. By the time we woke I felt only a little drained and a lot hungry. Empty — that covers both.

The door was not locked. That was a change. Wani and I found our way to the lab without an escort. I suppose, strictly speaking, she was my escort. No one else was up yet. Or maybe they were locked in. Only Nok was there. Working on his notes, I think, but he put them aside when we entered. "I have all the food here we brought up from your camp," he said. "Of course, now we know you can eat a Larnagian diet, feeding you will be simpler."

I turned to Wani. "You don't have any strange food habits, have you? No live worms or anything of that sort?" It was a joke but Wani didn't catch that and only solemnly shook her head.

I should learn her language. I wondered if that could be done with the machines here, the way we rapidly had Alienese poured into our brains. And Wani could finish learning English the same way. Hers was still a bit broken. I should ask.

I should also ask Nok how he was doing. He was a friend. I was fairly sure of that. "Are you and Pot going to be alright?" I asked. I figured that was about as neutrally and innocuously as I could put it.

"Neither of our spouses will be happy about this. *I'm* not happy and I'm sure Pot isn't. But accidents do happen."

"Couldn't you have restrained yourself?"

"And left her with unfertilized eggs? That would be a great cruelty."

I didn't know why it would be but decided to delve no deeper into Sormog sex. "Okay then," I said. "Let's fix some breakfast." I did wonder about those eggs Pot would be laying. Would there be little Sormogian wormlings crawling about the ship soon?

The rest of our party drifted in over the next few minutes. Donna and Mickie knew this place but it was new to Susan. If I'd been thinking clearly last night, I might have been able to do something for her. Even ask Wani to stay with her. Too late now.

She seemed okay. Susan always seemed to seem okay. Or so it seemed, ha-ha. It bugged me somewhat. But she had already hung around with Squid and Nok so what was a little space travel after that? And she could speak Alienese now, which might help.

Especially if none of us ever got home.

A rather strident voice erupted, in the squid language. Might that be the captain? I wasn't certain. Squid replied and turned on a viewer, running through a series of camera feeds. "Ah, there it is," he said.

'It' was a large humanoid figure, leaning against a metal wall somewhere. It looked like it might be a store room. He — it looked like a he — seemed rather the worse for wear, head drooping onto his folded arms. He looked up and shook that heavy-browed bearded head.

"Daddy!" cried Wani.

# Chapter 24

"WANI'S FATHER MUST have jumped aboard, just as we jumped. That left him quite disoriented, maybe unconscious," Nok told us. "It was only luck he didn't end up in space instead."

"Can you lock him up?" asked Susan.

"Think about it," I told her.

"Oh. Right." She frowned. "But you could knock him out. A sedative."

"He's too important for that sort of treatment, isn't he?" I asked. "If they went that far they might as well kill him. Not that they would, Wani," I hastened to reassure the girl. She had added nothing to the conversation, only watched her groggy father.

"So he is with us unless he decides to teleport somewhere."

"Which he won't," Mickie pointed out, "because we would immediately jump somewhere else and he'd never locate us again."

"I say, you all have a very good grasp on this," remarked Squid. "You are quite right. Nagudagdag will choose to remain with us."

"And we will have to risk offending him by not taking him wherever he thinks he should be. That might be almost as bad as sedating him, but what else can we do?" asked Nok.

"He will be a prisoner by his own choice," I said.

"Is someone going to go help him?" asked Wani. She seemed impatient and a bit peeved by our jabbering.

"On their way," Squid told her. "You, ah, know your father, um, male Larnagians — adult Larnagians — can have a temper and, um —"

The girl giggled. "And you're all afraid of him."

I think maybe I was too. "If you wait much longer, he'll come find you instead," I told them. And he was unlikely to be in a good mood about it.

"Ah, the captain must be speaking to our guest." Nagudagdag — yes, I remembered the name — was apparently listening to something. For some reason, Squid had chosen not to turn on the sound. Later I decided maybe the captain had ordered it. It would want its conversation with this high-up Larnagian to be private.

"He looks pissed," remarked Donna.

"He does," agreed Mickie. "Probably wants to see Wani."

"And he will. But he should not see any of you. Not right away," said Squid.

He was right. "You and I had better bunk separately for a while," I told Wani. "It would be safer."

The door to the room in which Nagudagdag sat slid open and a squid-star entered. Captain Squid himself, and an aide. "I should get down there and check him over," said the doctor. It rolled out of the lab.

"And the rest of you should disappear. It's likely to bring the Larnagian back here for his checkup." He considered Wani. "Hmm, maybe you too. He can see you soon enough."

No sooner did I get back to my room than the door opened. "The captain wants to see you," Mac informed me.

"All of us?"

"Just you and the Larnagian girl. She's already on the way." I couldn't expect any more explanation than that from Mac. It was pretty closed-mouth. All three of them.

I followed it up to the captain's control room. That's what I assumed it was. Wani was there, watching her dad on a screen, being gone over by Squid.

"We should speak," said the captain, "while Wani's father is being kept busy in the lab. This I must know: how did you choose this destination?"

"I just envisioned a place that would be good to live and went there."

"Extraordinary," it said. "I've never heard of such a thing, Wani."

She apparently hadn't either, so it continued. "We have a good fix on where we are now. Well outside of any area that has been previously explored. And, yes, the planet below us is a pretty good place for Larnagians or Earthlings to live. Survive, anyway. That could be improved over time."

It reached out a tentacle to turn on the sound from the lab. "How much longer?" the big Larnagian was grumbling. "I'd better see my daughter soon!"

"Why don't you go on down to him, Wani?" asked the captain. She nodded but didn't hurry on her way. The girl certainly would have reservations about talking to her father.

"You can watch with me," the captain told me. "I know this is important to you."

I sat down to watch the show. I could judge Nagudagdag's physical appearance better now, seeing him there beside Nok and Squid, and even better once Wani entered the lab. He was a big guy but not as big as my imagination had made him. I'd seen plenty of humans on Earth who were larger. He was six foot or so, deep-chested and muscular. Hairy but, again, no more so than many men. He did have the low forehead and heavy brow ridges one would expect from a Larnagian, and a massive jaw. Probably pretty much chinless beneath the thick beard.

His only clothes were a pair of shorts. Maybe he hadn't been dressed when he made his mad jump to our ship or maybe he just preferred to be casual. As he was the only male Larnagian I had yet seen, I can't tell you.

"At last," he roared, and pulled Wani into a fierce embrace. Then he stepped back to arms' length. "Who?" he said.

Wani only shook her head. I expected anger but instead he gave us weary exasperation. "Why not?" he asked. "I am not angry about this but I would like to meet my daughter's mate. And learn what another Larnagian was doing on this ship!" Of course, he would think a Larnagian was responsible. "Did you have a lover who jumped here to be with you?"

"No, Daddy. I — I can't tell you what happened. Not yet."

He scowled now and his scowl was a fearsome sight. "Well, he must be on board still. I know you didn't bring the ship here." The scowl turned to a chuckle. "Only a crazy male would make such a jump!"

The Larnagian turned to Nok and Squid. "I suppose you two won't tell me either. I'll have to take it up with the captain."

The captain whistled rather loudly. "Good luck with that. Maybe you should get back to your cabin, Dave. Don't show yourself for a while, alright?"

"Yes, sir." It was alright. Captain Squid was alright, too. I considered jumping to the room to avoid a chance meeting with Nagudagdag in a corridor but decided to use the elevator instead, riding down with Mac.

How had I managed to bring the ship here? I didn't have a clear idea at all of where I wanted to jump. I figured it would just be a random spot in space we could teleport away from again in a few hours. Yeah, I did 'see' a planet in my head so we would end up in a safe orbit rather than inside a star or something of that sort. Wani had filled me in on that sort of thing early on. Even before we knew I had this ability.

Not that any of this mattered. Not that I could see. Our primary problem remained, that of dealing with the Larnagians when they inevitably learned about us on Earth. And first we would have to deal with one Larnagian, here on this ship. What effect might that have on all that followed?

The door to my room slid open. There was nothing to do but wait. Wait and see. I was still tired and fell asleep almost at once.

# Chapter 25

"DADDY HAS A great deal of respect for you. He thinks you must be a very talented Larnagian. And a fearless one. That's more important to him!" Wani giggled. "I think he's going to be disappointed."

"If I was fearless I'd be in your room instead of looking at you on a screen," I replied. "I wonder how the others are holding up."

"Let's see." The view switched to Donna and Mickie's quarters. They seemed to be asleep. "Won't bother them," she said.

"I'd wondered if Susan had been put in the same room."

"They wouldn't like that."

"No, they wouldn't, but Susan would. She likes having someone to talk to."

"Then let's talk to her." A few seconds later Susan appeared on one half of the screen.

"Hey, guys," she said. "I've been figuring out how to use this contraption and looking around the ship. It's keeping me from going stir-crazy."

I'd have to remember to tape over my sensors again. "Anything interesting?" I asked.

"I've been peeking at Wani's father. I don't think he quite understands how to turn off the viewer."

"Daddy's not good with machines."

"So I can keep being a peeping Susan. I think he's kind of — well, sexy. Are he and your mom happy?"

Wani laughed outright. "Happy not to be together! She has another husband now." She then realized just what Susan meant. "Would you want to be one of his wives?"

"No, no, but he might be interesting to, um, sample. I mean, why should Dave be the only one with a Larnagian lover?"

I knew she was joking — pretty much — but Wani took all this quite seriously. "But he isn't supposed to know you are here."

"Don't worry. Susan isn't going to go down to his cabin and proposition your dear old dad."

"Not right now," added Susan.

"Umm, okay guys. Oh, I don't feel so good. Maybe I should go see —" Wani puked before she got any further. She gave us a wan smile and said, "The doctor."

Susan at once told her, "You might do better with Donna. She knows more about pregnant women."

Wani shot me a look. "Dave has made me sick again."

"Guilty," I agreed. "Need any help to clean that up?"

"Robot is already getting it. See?" She did something to the sensors at her end so we could glimpse a little box scuttling about the floor, removing any trace of the vomit. I wondered if one like that lurked somewhere in my own room. "Now I talk to Doctor Squid." With that she cut us off.

"This is quite a mess you've gotten all of us into," said Susan.

"Yeah, it was my fault I was abducted by aliens." I switched off the screen.

Then I was bored. Those feeds were the only entertainment here. Did the aliens have books? Not that I could read them but I wondered. Maybe movies of some sort. I must ask. I could look in at the lab. Nok or Squid could tell me.

That proved unnecessary. A short time later — an hour maybe? hard to tell on this ship — a short time later, Doctor Squid stopped by my room.

"What's up, Doc?" I greeted it. I had taken to calling it Doc recently, as I was getting to know too many other squids.

"I was visiting Wani," it told me, slipping into my cabin. "You are right about Donna being best qualified to tend to her. We'll have to work out some way to do it privately."

That seemed sensible and there wasn't much else to say about Wani except that she was holding up well enough. So I asked about movies.

"Yes, some species do have entertainments of that sort and some seem completely unable to understand their purpose. The Larnagians have a long and rich oral tradition, most of which has been recorded. Unfortunately, it is in languages you would not understand."

"I should probably learn Wani's native tongue one of these days."

"You already have. They speak what you call Alienese in everyday life on Ganc. Other languages are largely ceremonial."

I should have recognized that. Wani and her father did speak the pidgin to each other. "How's your other pregnant patient?" I asked. "Pot."

"Pregnant no more. She has laid three eggs and is fine now, but unlikely to emerge from her room through the rest of this journey. It is too warm in the ship."

"Oh, yes, you told me the cold had something to do with it all."

"It has everything to do with it. The Sormogian ancestors would mate when cold weather first came and then hole up through the winter. Not hibernate, exactly, but reduce their activity. Eggs would hatch by spring. These days, they can choose when they want to start a family, lowering the temperature in their habitations accordingly. Pot's room is kept cool now so she can rest and wait for the young ones to emerge.

"But Nok doesn't get to rest."

"No. He can't but he should. I understand it is fairly fatiguing for the males." A slight whistle followed. "It is, in fact, somewhat invigorating for my race to detach a lobe."

"Growing a new one must take some energy."

"Indeed. It makes one quite hungry. Would you like to view videos about the process?"

Squid porn? I didn't think so. "Maybe sometime. I'd be more interested in learning some cultural or political stuff. I think we all would. We know nothing of those worlds out there."

"I fear there would be little such in our library but I'll see what's available. We don't need it for what we do. Of course," it continued, "were emissaries sent to make open contact they would have all of that."

"So what do you have?" Doc Squid was being oblique. Perhaps it didn't want us to know too much or maybe it was just its nature.

"Popular amusements geared for our races, for the most part. You would not understand them at all. Wani may have some things you could enjoy. Human tastes and Larnagian tastes do not seem too dissimilar to me. But," it hastened to warn me, "do stay in your quarters for now."

I didn't intend to go traipsing down the hallways but if I jumped to another room it should be safe, shouldn't it? I had no plans to so I didn't mention it to Squid. "I promise not to step out of my door. So tell me about this planet I seem to have discovered."

"A nice place. Plenty of oxygen, which the majority of intelligent life prefers. Water too. The seas are a little iron-rich still. Temperate by your standards. To be honest, any number of species could make it their home with a little work. But," it continued, "the biology is very similar to that of Earth. Or Larnag. Some of the plants and animals are surely poisonous to your species but I suspect some are not. It is just the sort of place the first Larnagians might have discovered."

I could see why the captain was astonished. "So do I get to keep it?"

"That is something we are discussing." Which was not the response I had expected to my joke of a question.

Squid continued. "If it was decided to transplant some of you from Earth, this would be a good spot." It crouched there on its three legs for a moment, just looking at me. "I somehow doubt you are unusual, Dave. That would be too great a coincidence. Maybe anyone from Earth could have done the same. Anyone who can teleport."

It was right, of course. I was just a random guy they abducted. "This will make us seem all the more of a threat to the Larnagians."

"But it also gives us a handy bribe. They would certainly like a new hospitable planet to colonize."

"Then," I said, "maybe I'll just give it to them."

# Chapter 26

"I'M BORED," SAID Susan.

"Me too. How 'bout I visit?"

"But we're not supposed to leave our rooms. And mine is locked."

That last bit of info surprised me only a little. Our alien hosts might trust me but weren't so sure about Susan, I guess. "No problem," I told her. A moment later I had teleported into her quarters.

Accurately. I was kind of proud of that. "Your room is probably being monitored," I remarked. "They'll know I've visited."

She gave me a knowing smirk. "But you don't give a damn, right?"

"No, I don't and it gives them notice that they can't keep me contained. Or any of us." I spoke to the air. "You hear that guys? Don't fence me in!"

Susan only shook her head. "They can't fence *you* in. I'm another matter."

"Not so, Miss Rossi. Would you care to call on the Misses Vogel and Johanson?"

"Sure. Why not?"

"We'll have to leave Doo behind," I said and took her hand. A moment later we were with them. They probably should have been warned first but we didn't catch them doing anything naughty, so it was alright.

I sat down on their bed, a tad dizzy after two teleports in quick succession. Even if they were short jumps. And while I was sitting there I filled them in on everything I had learned.

"Won't any plans we make be heard?" asked Donna, her eyes flicking to the sensors. She'd figured out where they were.

I gazed at them somewhat nonchalantly. I could always put

some tape over them but I shouldn't say that now. "We have nothing to hide," I lied. Everyone has something to hide.

"By the way," I continued, "I find that Nok amassed a rather large catalog of Earth media we can access. He even has my recordings."

"Including the song Mickie hates?" asked Donna.

"It's just misunderstood," I maintained. "There's a Larnagian library too, stuff Wani apparently enjoys. Haven't had a chance to check it out."

Susan began to fiddle with the viewer controls. "I've figured out some of the symbols," she told us, over her shoulder. "I might be able to find it. Hmm, I think this is it. That's the word for Larnagian." She pointed out an Alienese script on the screen.

"Damn, your ex is smart," remarked Donna.

"You're not telling me anything. Find something interesting?"

"Don't know. I'll just try out entries at random." The first image to fill the screen was a pageful of words. "That looks like the same kind of writing they use here on the ship," she said. "We're not going to figure it out." She tried another entry.

"A movie! Let's watch," said Mickie. We didn't watch long. It was essentially porn. And not good porn.

"I suppose you need something like that when you're stuck on a ship light years away from your kind," was Donna's opinion. "But who would have guessed there were Larnagian porn actors?"

"I hope they were actors," was all I had to say. "Um, the guys were kind of, um —"

"Under-endowed? I think we all noticed," said Susan. "Even compared to you." Ah, there was the Susan I knew of old.

"Oh," chortled Mickie, "so that's why little Wani seduced you!"

There might be some truth to it. She had been watching me in my room. "Anything else we can try to watch?"

The next video Susan pulled up consisted mainly of female Larnagians talking for quite some time. There didn't seem to be much of a thread to their conversation. Then a male showed up and it turned into porn again.

"I think we'll give up on Larnagian movies," said Susan. We all agreed and spent the next couple hours sampling some of the stuff Nok had accumulated. We were watching one of Attenborough's nature documentaries when Squid's voice broke in.

"Those are rather good, aren't they? Your people do interesting work. And it saves us research time! Would you like all your dinners delivered to the one room?"

I looked around. Susan shook her head. "I think we're done hanging for a while, Squid. I'll get Susan and myself back to our own rooms."

"Very well, Dave. I wish you wouldn't jump around the ship but I admit you're not actually breaking your promise." And there was no way it could prevent me. It knew that.

After eating in my room I felt bored again. Probably Susan did too but she knew how to access Larnagian porn now. I missed Wani. It was true.

I got her on the viewer but we didn't have much to say. "I'm just sitting in my quarters too," she told me. "I wish you were with me."

Why not? "Lights out," I mouthed. She didn't get it. So I pointed to my own lights and told them to turn off. A moment later, her room was dark too.

Not that it mattered if anyone watched me pop in to visit Wani. Unless it was her dad. I didn't know if he had access to a viewer or even knew how to use one. The alien crew definitely would be preventing him from seeing into any human-occupied rooms.

I was with her at once. And I had tape. It was nice just to be there with her, to snuggle against her. I wondered about our child. Was Donna right? Could our genetic differences keep it from being viable or effect its health if it did survive the pregnancy? I even wondered if it would look like its grandfather Nagudagdag.

All that would be as it would be. The same way things had been since all this started. We fell asleep there, in Wani's room, in Wani's bed, my arm around her.

"Wani?" asked a deep voice. It was coming from the viewer. Her father, to be sure, and he wouldn't be able to see a thing in the room. "Are you there?"

Her answer was a sleepy "Huh?" I figured I'd better teleport out of there right then.

Suddenly, the voice was in the room, not in the viewer. "Lights on! Full!" Of course, Nagudagdag could teleport in just as readily as I could go out. He frowned at me from beneath those beetling brows. Maybe I should jump anyway. No, best to stay here. I shouldn't desert Wani.

"Who is this?" he asked. "*What* is this?"

"Oh, Daddy. Hi." She sat up. "This is Dave. He's the father of my baby!"

Nagudagdag glared at me again and I didn't like it one bit.

# Chapter 27

"MOST OF THEM can *not* teleport. It is a relatively rare ability on Earth."

One in ten wasn't really rare but I could see why Squid would shadow the truth a little.

"But some can," muttered Nagudagdag. "You think my ancestors came from this Earth planet. Why did we change so much?" He gave me yet another looking over. There had been a lot of them, as if he couldn't quite believe I existed.

"They are the ones who changed. Larnagians have remained surprisingly close to their original form." Squid turned to me. "You may have been right with the heidelbergenis hypothesis, Dave, from what genetic evidence we've found. Or quite possibly a step or two closer to what you humans consider modern."

"Well, I knew we came from somewhere." The big guy laughed. "I am not one to believe Nuvu created us on Larnag. I am educated."

And a pretty smart Larnagian, I guessed. Maybe he could be reasoned with. "I hope we can get a fresh start now, Nagudagdag," I said, "now that you know about me."

"Dagdag," he said. "Nagu is the family name."

"So your daughter is Naguwani?"

He looked puzzled. "Who ever heard of females having family names? Until they are married, of course."

Was that a hint? I wasn't quite sure whether he wanted me as son-in-law or not. The captain rejoined the conversation. "I think you should go down and take a look at Planet Dave. Both of you."

Planet Dave was flattering. I was not nearly as pleased with the idea of teleporting down there with this guy.

"By saucer shuttle, of course," added Squid. "We've been down several times, gathering samples and data."

That would be better. "We should all go down and take a look. Wani too."

So it was arranged. All the humans, both Larnagians. I was surprised that the captain came along. I guess they didn't actually need him on a ship in orbit. Nok accompanied us but not Doc. And Susan had to leave Doo behind. He had been following her about the ship and growling occasionally at one alien or another.

Dagdag was in his shorts again. He had worn an ill-fitting jumpsuit the last I had seen him. I assumed the ship didn't have one in his extra-large size. He said nothing as we descended. As before, I felt little of the ride. Even the entry to the planet's atmos-phere was smooth.

We set down on a hillside, among rocks. Every place else was thick with a riot of vegetation. Below us towered trees that would rival the greatest of redwoods. I call them trees but assume they had no relation to those on Earth. Nothing here would. It would have followed its own evolutionary path.

Yet Squid had said its chemistry was close enough to ours to perhaps be compatible. I breathed in the rich air. It was good to be away from the stink of the ship!

Susan took it all in for a minute or two. "I don't think this place should be named Planet Dave," she said. "I suggest Paradise."

The word she used wasn't paradise, strictly. It was an Alienese word that had approximately the same meaning. "Some of my race think that your planet is Paradise," said Dagdag. "The distant home we left, long ago, and could never find again."

"Maybe it was, once," murmured Donna.

"And maybe we can start over here," came Mickie's reply.

Donna gave her an astonished look. "You and me?"

"If you want." Mickie laughed. "I meant humans in general."

"Maybe Larnagians too," I added.

There was a lake in the distance, or maybe a sea. What creatures might dwell in its depths? What roamed that great forest? I looked up to see if aught flew through the skies. I admit to being disappointed that I saw nothing.

Nagudagdag jumped up onto one of the rocks and surveyed this world. "This puts Ganc to shame. I wonder if Larnag was once so."

"Or Earth," whispered Susan. "When there were men like Dagdag roaming it."

Said Dagdag roared out, "I would have this world as my own! Mine and my people's."

"Perhaps," said the captain, "something can be arranged. First, we must work out the problem of Earth."

He leaped down. "Problem?"

"Of them being possible rivals to the Larnagians. There are those who fear you will hurt them."

Nok quickly added, "Not you. Your people, if they think those of Earth are a threat."

"Some might," Dagdag admitted.

Captain Squid went on. "I could see some members of your society jumping there without thought and attacking individuals."

"Males, you mean. Yes, that is possible."

"Especially young restless ones. I would fear an organized attack more. That is what we must prevent." Dagdag actually looked thoughtful as he listened to this. "Larnagians, on their own, couldn't eliminate the people of Earth, of course. They could certainly disrupt things. That would serve no purpose for anyone."

"No, it would not. The Council is considering all this, isn't it?"

"Indeed they are. We have been trying to give them time."

"And so Wani hid from me." He nodded his massive head. "I

understand. I must speak to the Council. First I will look over more of this place. Walk with me, Wani."

"Me too," said Susan and followed them.

We watched the trio wander down the hillside. The captain turned to the rest of us and said, "It is true the Larnagians, individually or even in a mass attack — rioting, if you will — could cause considerable damage. But they might also get hold of ships and tools that could do far worse things to your planet. They wouldn't really have to know how to use them that well."

"And it would be hard for us to prevent them," said Nok.

"Less so now that we have a couple humans who can navigate," the captain pointed out. "They could bring at least a few ships to protect Earth. Better, though," it said, its eye stalks directed to me, "if we also have some Larnagians on your side."

"We have one," I said. "Let's hope we can persuade another."

Donna turned her eyes toward the now distant Dagdag and the two women. "I think Susan is working on that."

I had to chuckle. "Yeah, she is, isn't she?"

# Chapter 28

"WAS HE LIKE those other male Larnagians we saw?" asked Donna.

"Oh, yes. It was really quite itsy-bitsy."

"Those poor Larnagian girls," was Donna's response to that. "Not that it matters to me, of course, Mickie. Not at all."

It was hard to tell how serious she was being. Mickie ignored the remark.

"Ummm." Nok wanted to say something but didn't seem sure he should. "That is fairly, um, normal for Larnagians. It seems you Earth humans are much better endowed. In fact — um, in fact, Squid and I have debated whether that was why Wani first decided to, um, visit you, Dave."

"I don't blame her at all," said Susan. "Isn't that what you suggested, Mickie?"

"Yeah." That was all she was willing to say and that came reluctantly.

"Dave's not so bad otherwise, either. Yeah, I'll admit it." She gave the Sormog a looking over. "Whatever god created you didn't skimp in that department, did he? No wonder Larnagian girls have sometimes fantasized about you guys."

"I can not be accountable for other species," Nok replied.

"I 'spose not. Daggy's actually not bad in the sack. Enthusiastic, anyway." She smirked. "And Doo likes him. That's always a must."

She was starting to go on just a little too much about this. That was Susan. She didn't know when to quit.

Fortunately for both of us, I had known when to quit.

"Are we ever going to go home?" burst out Mickie, of a sudden.

"I don't think any of us know," I said. I wasn't all that sure I wanted to but I wasn't going to say that.

"Paradise doesn't seem so bad," said Donna. "Do we have anything we really need to go back for, Mick?"

Mickie didn't answer but Susan did. "I do. My life is there, such as it is."

"I think we should be able to return those who wish it," spoke Nok. "One can't be certain, of course. We intend to orbit here a while longer. There is much to learn about Paradise, as you have named it — that will probably stick, officially, by the way." There was a pause. "But more importantly it gives us a chance to work things out with Nagudagdag. It is good you are keeping him happy, Susan."

She sputtered but held whatever reply she might have thought to make.

It was Donna who said, "It might be more important that Wani and Dave keep him happy. By the way, I am sure that Doc knows the gender of their kid. Has it told anyone?"

Heads were shaken all around, and antennae twitched. "It most likely didn't even think about it," felt Nok. "I am afraid our squid friends, despite their familiarity with us, do not really understand gender and its importance."

"I'd be happy with either," said Donna. "If I were having a child, I mean." She gave Mickie a sidelong glance. "Maybe when we get home we can talk about that again."

"And if we don't?" asked her girlfriend. She suddenly grinned. "The only man available for millions of miles is Dave!"

"There are always Larnagians," Susan pointed out.

"I think I would prefer Dave," said Donna. "That is, if we are stuck out here."

"Yeah," agreed Mickie, giving me the sort of look I might a

plate of cold French fries. "You know, Dave, it's not like I find the idea loathsome or you repulsive. I'm just not very interested in sex with guys." She shrugged. "I suppose it still feels good and I could always use my imagination."

I had to laugh at that, though a fleeting image of a threesome with her and Donna slipped in and out of my head. "I would think our alien scientists could come up with a scheme for artificial impregnation, if you really wanted to do it. But not now," I added, addressing Nok.

"Understood. You would be their last resort." I'm pretty sure he meant it as a joke. It was also true.

A faint whir as the door to the lab slid open. Squid preceded our two Larnagians into the room. Wani at once came to me. Dagdag looked like he might want to do the same with Susan but held back.

Was this big guy, a supposed leader of his people, actually shy around women? Or maybe just shy around Susan. He wouldn't be the first. He might even be intimidated by a woman far smarter than any he had ever known.

Not that the Larnagian was stupid. Among his own people, he might well have prided himself on his intelligence. And, as his daughter, he would be somewhat average in the brains department back on Earth.

This was what had come to worry me the most about the Larnagians. Not just that they would see us as rivals because some of us could teleport but the fact that we were smarter. Already, they knew they weren't as bright as the other alien races out there. To have us outstrip them as well might simply be too much.

"It is a very good world," Dagdag was enthusing. "We should bring animals from Ganc."

"From Earth, too," I said. "And crop plants."

"Dogs," added Susan.

His heavy brow furrowed in thought. "But which of our peoples will live here?"

"Why not both?" I asked. "Wani and I have already made a start on that, you might say." I realized at that moment I did want to stay here, on this new world. Earth held nothing for me anymore.

The big Larnagian let his eyes rest on Susan for just a moment, almost bashfully. "Why not both?" he agreed.

# Chapter 29

SUSAN AND I had come up separately from the others. We were both tired of wandering around on the planet. We'd been doing that a couple weeks now. I would have thought at first there were wonders enough to hold our interest for a lifetime, the emeralds and beryls and opals of the riotous vegetation, the clear sapphire sky, the burnished gold of towering peaks, but we wanted to get to *doing* something.

I could come and go as I wished, being able to teleport. If I paced myself it wasn't that draining, and taking someone along with me didn't seem to make a difference. We were sitting in the lab with Nok now, sipping beer. I wondered how much was still on board.

"He keeps popping in every night," Susan was saying. "Sometimes during the day. A teleporting lover is a pretty big nuisance!"

"Hmm." Nok looked at her a moment before going to one of the lockers and pulling out a small device. "I should probably leave this to the doctor," he muttered, apparently to himself, as he waved it toward Susan. "Yes, yes. Pregnant, though naturally the embryo isn't implanted yet. We could rid you of it if you wish."

"Oh, hell," was her only comment.

"If you do, make it now," I advised. "Before Dagdag learns about it."

She nodded. "I need to think about this."

She'd never thought about it while we were together. Susan had used birth control throughout our relationship. Maybe she'd run out of pills or something — it was kind of far to the closest pharmacy.

"Walk with me to my room, will you?" she asked.

"Sure." I nodded a goodbye to Nok and accompanied her out the door. "No more teleporting for you if you keep it," I informed her as we passed down the corridor. There would be fifty-fifty chance the child would be able to teleport, wouldn't there? No point in bringing that up until she had made her decision.

At her doorway she turned and said to me, "I decided to go off the pill when I drove up to White Springs. Honestly, Dave, I'd decided I wanted a baby before it was too late and, well, I'd as soon have had you as the father as anyone. You hadn't told me about Wani."

"You planned to seduce me, Miss Rossi?"

"It's not so hard to do. But when I got there I could see it was not a good idea for either of us."

Susan was in her mid-thirties, a couple years younger than me. I thought I could understand. Not completely, but some, you know? Human feelings are human feelings.

"Dagdag might not be such a bad choice as a father. Whether he knows about it or not."

"Yeah. But maybe best if I can get home before it shows." Susan gave me an almost-grin. "It may be a homely kid. But being mine, people would expect that." She went in and the door slid shut behind her.

Did that mean she intended to keep it? It certainly seemed like she was leaning that way. Ha, if she stayed with Nagudagdag she would be my mother-in-law, wouldn't she? Sort of. I really should get Wani to fill me in on Larnagian marriage customs. If there was some ceremony, I was ready. Ready to make it official.

Here I was making plans when all was still very much up in the air. There was no guarantee of a 'happily ever after' for any of us. Not that there ever is. I wandered about the ship a while. No one cared about that anymore. The crew was used to me, as well as being aware I could teleport anywhere. They were pretty evenly divided, that crew, between squid-stars and Sormogs, and I could never see that their species had any bearing on their occupations.

I could see that the ship was designed for them and their two very different body shapes and sizes. That every ship carried a Larnagian as well meant there were also concessions to my own shape and size. There were other shapes and sizes out there in the universe, scores of them, and I would see some of them sooner or later.

Not that I could say I was eager to. There was definite apprehension about the whole thing. Who was I to go speak with them for the human race? Dave Ladd, a middle-aged musician, never quite famous enough to rank as a has-been? Earth could do a hell of a lot better.

I found my way to Gof's workshop, which connected with what I thought of as the engine room. I'm not sure it actually was. Gof was Sormogian, male, and thicker through than any others I had seen. Whether he was naturally robust or Sormogs simply got fat, I didn't — and don't — know.

All our stuff was there, some of it dismantled, some whole, some out, some stowed away. "Hey, Gof," I said, "I wanted to see if I can get one of my guitars."

"Guitars? The sound-makers? Over here." I followed him. "What are they used for?"

"To make sound, of course." I thought better of the joke and added, "They are for music."

"Ah. I do not understand Earth music."

I had heard Sormogian music and did not understand it, so we were even. As far as I could tell, each piece consisted of one droning note. I chose the old Ovation, first checking that the rest of the instruments were intact. Maybe I should grab Susan's banjo too, I decided. She might like to play while she thought. Or play so she didn't have to think. Both work.

I headed back to her quarters with both instruments, walking, not teleporting. Mac was outside her door. "You are all to see the captain," it reported. I left both banjo and guitar in Susan's room and we followed it. Doo padded along behind us.

"We're going to the lab?" I asked.

"We are."

Captain Squid waited there, along with Doc and Nok, both Larnagians, both human women. They had been waiting on us.

The captain had but one announcement. "We are done here. It is time to jump home."

# PART IV. PARADISE

## Chapter 30

"WANI IS OUT, of course, and Mickie and you don't know your way around the universe well enough," the captain explained. "So Nagudagdag must serve as navigator." I did not get the impression it was pleased with this.

"We could find the way back to Earth, I'm sure. Either one of us."

"I have considered this. It is likely at least one ship remains there with a Larnagian who could go fetch us another navigator. But I won't chance revealing your abilities before we are prepared."

"They'll have to know eventually." Dagdag certainly wasn't going to keep his mouth shut forever.

"This is so." It seemed to ponder for a while. Why did the captain choose to impart this information to me and not the others? Did it see me as the leader, the spokesperson for his little group of humans? "There is a saying of your race, 'look before you leap,' is there not? Males like Nagudagdag have a tendency to do the opposite." It whistled a laugh. "Perhaps you do, as well."

"We're reckless," I said.

"Which is a danger with a clumsy jumper. Nagudagdag is skillful enough. He will have to serve."

That was its decision, to be sure, and quite possibly the correct one. "So where are we to go?"

It brought up what I assumed was a chart on one of the screens. I couldn't make a whole lot of sense of it. "We'll make the long jump to this system first." It pointed it out with a tentacle. "That will get us into Connected space. Then we'll work our way to wherever the Council is currently meeting. The exact route will be up to our navigator, though I shall certainly make suggestions."

"Are all navigators young females then?" I asked. "The males aren't trustworthy at all?" I wasn't sure I could believe there was that much difference between the sexes. But they weren't Earth humans. I couldn't judge them accordingly.

"Some males are perfectly good at it and have long careers. Longer than most of the females. But the talented ones," it continued, "tend to end up on courier duty, teleporting from planet to planet on their own. Our Nagudagdag served so when young."

I could buy that. I could also see those young male Larnagians vying with each other to make long and dangerous leaps. I was beginning to figure them out — and realize they were a lot more like us than they were different.

The teleport would not occur for a couple hours. I spread the news to the others and then had nothing to do but wait. "Is your father ready?" I asked Wani eventually.

"I haven't seen him."

Odd, he typically spent a lot of time with her. When he wasn't spending time with Susan. "Maybe he's with the captain," I said. "Let's see."

We went up a deck. The operation of this vessel was pretty casual and no one minded if we poked our noses into the captain's control center. "Oh," it said, as soon as it saw us, "Nagudagdad is just about ready. We've been discussing the jump." Early. He must be eager to go.

The Larnagian was settling himself into the navigator's chair. "I'm ready." It came almost as a growl. Dagdag seemed edgy.

The captain announce the jump to his crew and gave him the

go-ahead. A moment later Captain Squid was checking its instruments. "That's not our target below us," it said.

"No, it is not," Nagudagdag agreed, and disappeared.

The captain took only a few seconds to get its bearings. "We're above Ganc."

"Damn," I said, and slipped into the navigation chair. "Get ready to go again right now!"

To its credit, Captain Squid did as I demanded. A few moments later we were above Earth. It seemed the surest and safest jump. "We shouldn't stay here too long," I told it. "Dagdag may come after us."

"With more Larnagians. He intended to come back and try to take over the ship, didn't he?" said the captain. It is good you saw that at once."

"And claim Paradise." Dagdag might well have pulled it off, given a little longer to organize back on Ganc. It would take a while to round up even a handful of followers.

"He could still do that," Wani pointed out.

"And so we must get to the Council as quickly as possible. Are you up to another jump, Dave?"

"I'll have to be," I replied, and settled back into the chair.

# Chapter 31

"WHY DIDN'T DAGDAG do that while we are at Paradise?" asked Donna. "He could have jumped home anytime."

"Only he could be sure of knowing the way back," Wani told her. "A ship orbiting Ganc is another matter. Easy to see." She frowned. "I am very angry with my father!"

I was a bit peeved myself. I did have to admit it was a rather well put together plan. Given a few minutes more he might have pulled it off.

Or maybe not. There were a lot of things that could have gone wrong. One was me being in the control room and realizing what had happened. And what could he hope to accomplish long-term? Get a few Larnagians onto Paradise?

Mickie had taken over after I teleported the ship in the general direction the captain had indicated. I hit the right system but kind of far out. She got us into orbit at the right planet. Otherwise, it would have taken days of using the ship's engines to get us there and I was admittedly too drained to go again right away.

We were able to communicate in that system and learn where the Council currently was meeting. "As expected," the captain said, "but it's best to check. I wouldn't want you jumping millions of miles the wrong direction." A couple more teleports and we were there.

Mickie and I both agreed it got easier to picture our destination each time, when we compared notes after. "If everything else goes to hell, we can always find jobs," she said.

"Oh, I was expecting Wani to support me after the baby came." She was the wrong audience for that joke. I think Mickie was the wrong audience for me, period.

No matter. I was to accompany Squid and Nok down to speak with this Council of theirs, or members of it anyway. I got the feeling all this was rather unofficial. "The captain wants Mickie to remain aboard just in case there is a need to suddenly teleport the ship," Doc Squid told me. "Would you prefer Susan or Donna accompany you?"

"Donna," I said. I didn't need to think about it. She was the most level-headed one of us.

We were about to take a saucer down to Whiz-whiz-gulp-whiz (which is the best I can do with the planet's name) when Mac came scuttling up. "There's been a security breach," it announced. "Captain wants you." We followed it back up two levels to the command center.

Without any preliminaries, the captain announced, "We had an intruder, a Larnagian. She must have jumped aboard when we paused at Earth." It brought up her image on a screen.

"That's Wani's friend," remarked Donna. "What's-her-name."

"Muca. And not a friend anymore, I think. Is she still aboard?"

"Teleported away before we knew she was here. But she accessed all the notes on your people first." He changed the screen to display her doing just that, in Nok and Squid's lab.

Nok stared at it. "She knew where to go and what to look for. It demonstrates surprising intelligence."

"So she's a genius among Larnagians," I said. "The question is what she plans to do with the information."

"Hand it over to someone higher up?" asked Donna.

"Quite likely," said the captain. "Someone on Larnag."

"We're not going to be a secret any longer," I observed. "The question now is how the Larnagians will act. Do they know about this down below?"

"The information has been relayed. Now you should be, as well."

We took that as a dismissal and hurried back to the shuttle. Shortly, we were dropping through the planet's thick atmosphere. "That's not breathable for you and me," Doc informed us. "Nok could handle it a while."

"But it's way too cold," said the Sormog. "We won't go outside. The Council chamber will have a suitable atmosphere."

"Except we're not going to meet with the full Council. Not enough time," the doctor told him. It was news to Nok. "A private meeting and quick action is called for."

"Does this Council, um, rule the universe or something?" asked Donna.

"It coordinates the member worlds of the Connected Systems. Mostly in matters of trade," explained Nok. "The Council avoids getting involved in politics as much as possible."

Which would sometimes be impossible. As now.

The saucer landed in some sort of hangar. I could see the the murky purplish-brown atmosphere all around us. How would we get indoors? A tube? Space suits? I'd seen too many ideas in sci-fi movies.

What they used was a bus, for want of a better word. It locked onto our door, we got in, it took us away. A simple and sensible way to do it. Maybe the quickest way too, but I wished it were quicker yet. Who knew what was happening on Paradise or on Earth? If the Larnagians wanted, they could make everyone blind to what was happening elsewhere. Everyone but Mickie and me.

There were those 'new' aliens I expected to see inside. I had too much on my mind to pay them close attention. A couple of them were humanoid. Or larnagoid, as our alien friends would put it. One looked like a rather large spider, but with more legs. Too many legs! We were hurried along, down a hall with crystalline-like walls, pale blue.

Our guide was a familiar squid-star. Yes, familiar and almost comforting by this point, amid the novelties and strangeness of this place. Perhaps that was intended. It led us to a translucent door. "Enter," it requested. "I remain here."

I decided I should be the first in. It was purely a decision of the moment, a whim, even, but the future of humanity was going to be addressed so humanity had best assert itself. I led the others into a modest room with the same crystal walls. The one at the far side was completely clear and the thick planetary atmosphere swirled beyond. I thought it a window to the outside.

No, a figure, two figures, appeared at it. Another room, suited to the natives. Or maybe some other aliens with similar biology. I had no way of knowing.

"Wouldn't a viewer have been more practical?" I whispered to Nok.

"Practicality is not a concern here," he replied. "The symbolism of meeting face to face is more important to some races. Those are our hosts." Nok would know these things. They were pretty much his specialty.

They looked like badly-made balloon animals, with a tangle of yarn glued on top. The other occupants of the room came to only three, one of them vaguely humanoid or perhaps more like a four-limbed stick insect. On one side of it sat something like a six-legged bear; on the other, crouched one of those multi-legged spider-things.

"I am Nac-nac-nac-nac," insect-man announced, "head of this committee. We have been given complete emergency authority to deal with this situation," it said. She said, I decided.

"And quite a situation it is," I replied. "So what do we do?"

# Chapter 32

"I'm inclined to believe we should deal with Paradise first and then take up the issue of Earth," I told them. We had been only laying out what was what up to that point.

"Why so?" asked the spider. It spoke with one of the most beautiful voices I had ever heard.

"It is a smaller problem and can be gotten out of the way first if we move quickly. And," I added, though I felt rather unsure about it, "I am not sure Nagudagdag is necessarily our, um, enemy in this. He was hoping to get himself into a strong bargaining position." That was what I had come up with after pondering what had happened. I knew I could be completely wrong.

Donna spoke up, which I had not expected at all. "And if we control Paradise it gives us that stronger bargaining position ourselves, both with Ganc and Larnag."

"This is so," agreed Nac-nac-nac-nac. She and her companions conferred in low voices for a moment, which I felt was a tad rude. "So how do you propose dealing with Nagudagdag and the Paradise question?"

"We'll lead ships there," I said. "Me and the other human who can teleport. As many as we can as long as we can, before Nagudagdag can get enough followers there to take possession."

"If you have ships ready," spoke Nok for the first time.

"We have had them ready for quite some time," spider-creature said. "Ever since this whole affair first came to our attention. When you sent the Larnagian girl with your preliminary findings."

"How is the girl?" asked the bear. "And where are her loyalties in this?" It's voice did not match it any better than the spider's, being rather high and shrill.

"Wani's loyalties are with me," I told them.

"Which is to be expected of a female in her culture," added Nok. "Her allegiance would be to her mate and his, um, tribe."

"Or you could just say she loves this guy," Donna said.

"Can she guide ships too?"

I shook my head. "Not when she is pregnant."

"So only two," murmured the chairwoman. "I am for this."

The other committee members agreed at once. I don't know what the balloons on the other side of the window thought and it probably didn't matter. The door opened. "Escort these Earth people to the ships at once," she told the waiting squid and turned back to us. "This was what we anticipated as our action but we needed to know you were willing first. May fortune be with you."

The doctor said at once when we were in the hall, "Mickie needs to come down as quickly as possible. In the saucer; there is no point in wasting her energy on a jump. I'll go fetch her." It hurried off toward the hangar, Donna following. We hurried off in a different direction.

"You're going to stay with me?" I asked Nok.

"I would seem best qualified to coordinate." He said no more for a few seconds, as we followed in the path of the scuttling squid-star. "It will be dangerous jumping back here without a ship. I know this. Especially the first time. You'll be less certain of your target."

"I know. I'm worried about Mickie." She didn't have to volunteer, to be sure, and maybe she wouldn't. "And the first time will be tricky, sure. I'm also concerned about later jumps when we are fatigued. We'll have to push ourselves to get enough ships there." I wondered just how many the Connected Systems had standing ready.

Two long teleports for each ship we took to Paradise. Divided by two if we were both able to keep it up. I'd just have to see. "Where are these ships?" I asked our guide.

"In orbit," it replied. "We'll take a shuttle up to the first."

"That makes sense," said Nok.

"But it will slow things down." I was in a hurry to get going.

"A shuttle ride after each jump back here will give you a little time to recuperate," he observed. "You would want to teleport into this building on your return trip."

"Hmm, I suppose so." That would be the sensible path. "But if, say, you or Squid was on the next ship to go, I might be able to see you and jump right to it."

The twitching of his antennae certainly signaled agitation. "Far too dangerous. Don't go acting like a male Larnagian."

I could only laugh at that. "Good advice, my friend."

"I am your friend," stated Nok.

"Very well, instead you should stay in the shuttle and I'll try to jump right back to it, ready to go up to the next ship. Maybe Doc could do the same for Mickie."

Our guide announced that we had arrived. It was another hanger, and another bus took us to another saucer. Soon enough, I was in the navigator's chair of an unfamiliar ship. The captain was of a race I didn't recognize. I'd probably be seeing a lot of that.

Paradise. I'd jumped there before, albeit not really knowing where I was headed. It wasn't hard to see it in my head, the spot to bring us into orbit, and then we were there.

"No other ships," someone reported to the captain. I nodded and prepared to teleport back. Take a couple breaths, Dave. It was a long jump. Go!

Whoa! I was in the hangar but there was no shuttle. I'd beaten it back to the planet. At once I teleported myself beyond the doors, into the building, choking on the one breath of that noxious atmosphere. Between that and three quick jumps I was kind of knocked silly and sank to my knees.

A squid immediately came up to me. I'm pretty sure it was the one who accompanied Nok and me here. Maybe left to guard the hangar, keep the curious away. "Do you need aid?" it asked.

I coughed a few times before answering. "I guess not. What the heck is in that air out there?"

"Nothing too poisonous, I've been assured. Heavy on carbon dioxide, some methane."

"Even so, I think I will aim for this spot the next time. It will help me see it if you remain here."

"Then I shall do so," it declared. A few minutes later the shuttle appeared and I felt up to going off to another ship.

"Mickie has made her first teleport," Nok informed me. "She is going to use our ship as her return point rather than the planet."

"Good idea," I grunted. We wouldn't see each other in passing then. It might have been easier on us if we could have commiserated between jumps. "Have you heard how many ships are waiting up there?"

It twitched one antennae. "I haven't heard but I saw them as we approached in the saucer. There might be as many as a hundred."

Wow, this Council really had been prepared. "I hope they all have breathable air," I said. But if they depended on Larnagians to navigate them, they would also have arrangements for them to breath. I jumped three more ships to Paradise before I collapsed and slept. I hoped Mickie did as well.

# Chapter 33

WHEN I WOKE up I started again. I think I slept no more than two or three hours. Ship after ship, jump after jump. I stopped when I must, when fatigue and, more important, disorientation became too much.

During a rest period, Nok told me, "Already many of the Larnagian navigators have disappeared. There is little doubt they were called home so ships could not move between the stars."

So we were needed more than ever, Mickie and me. "Do the Larnagians have ships?" I asked.

"You mean ships equipped for teleportation, I am sure, and the answer is of course they do. Some. Many Larnagians don't see the point when they can jump anywhere without them."

"Hmm, okay. I think I'm ready to go again."

And so we went on. I think I ended up taking as many as thirty ships to Paradise before we called a halt. I had lost track early on, concentrating only on getting one more ship there and getting myself back, only to do it again.

"We are going up to our own ship this time," Nok had informed me as I returned once more. "One of you can jump it to Paradise when you are ready."

I wasn't thinking that straight right then but I realized something had happened. "Why?"

"Mickie reports that some sort of agreement has been reached with Nagudagdag. That's all I know. Except that we don't need to hurry."

Mickie didn't really know anything more, either, when I saw her. She looked awful. I'm sure I did too, though maybe not as awful as I felt. "I'll flip you for which one has to make the teleport," I offered.

"I'm not about to be flipped, Mister," she muttered. "Let me sleep a day or two and then we'll decide."

As it was, she was still asleep when I awoke so I teleported us all to Paradise. There was the Connected fleet, over fifty ships, orbiting the planet. As I sank back, weary still, in the navigation chair, the captain said, "I am told the Larnagians had a couple ships here, as well as a handful of men. They actually made a sortie against one of our ships at one point but the numbers were just too much for them to win."

"Even with their ability to teleport." A landing party of Larnagians could suddenly materialize inside any ship. That was a scary thought.

"They could be a danger to a ship like this," it replied. "Not so much to one with a large well-trained crew ready to defend it."

Soldiers? Policemen? I needed to know a lot more about these Connected worlds. "I should probably rest some more," I said. "And find Wani!"

"I should think so. You have the gratitude of many for what you and Mickie did these past days. Perhaps you should have the gratitude of your home planet but they are unlikely to ever know."

I wasn't completely sure what it was implying with that. I let it go and meandered in the direction of my quarters. No, I decided, I'll stop in the lab and steal some of my alien friends' booze. I deserved it and then some.

Everyone was there. Even Mickie, looking a tad more rested. Wani flung her arms around me. "You are a hero!" she proclaimed. "Mickie is a hero! I have watched her push herself. I — I don't think I could have. Not like her."

"You never know until you need to know," I answered. "So who is in all these ships we've been bringing anyway? If they made Dagdag back down, they have my respect."

Squid answered. "Most are security forces from one system or another, not really used to this sort of thing. The elite here is from the Connection Patrol, which primarily concerns itself with pirates."

"Pirates." I thought on that. "There would have to be Larnagians involved in that, wouldn't there?"

"Larnagians have been known to engage in piracy. That is, navigate for pirates, mostly. Petty theft is much more common for them, jumping aboard a ship, grabbing something, and jumping away again. It's something young males sometimes do just for the thrill or as a dare."

I had to chuckle. "That does not surprise me at all. You'll find similar behavior among young males on Earth."

"Fortunately," said Doc, "they can not teleport."

"Not yet," I reminded him. When they learned how, the Connection Patrol might have its hands full. "Anyway, this fleet did the job. I'm glad Mickie and I were able to help."

Donna wasn't having that. She put her arm around her girl-friend. "More than help. Wani's dad would have gotten away with it if you hadn't got them here."

"My father is going to come up to negotiate soon," Wani said. "He insisted we be here first."

"Speaking of your father, do I need to ask him for your hand in marriage?"

She tipped her head at me. "What a silly idea! What does Daddy have to do with it? But of course," she continued, "you must bring many valuable gifts to my mother, before you beg her to allow us to marry."

I quite believed her. It was Squid's whistle that gave her away. "Maybe I should just be asking you, Wani."

"That's a good idea too. When are you going to do it?"

"Soon."

"Idiot," said Susan.

"Okay, now. Will you be my wife, Wani?"

"Yep. It was about time we got that out of the way."

"You'll need a priestess, right?" asked Nok. Almost apologetically, he explained, "I've been looking into Larnagian customs."

"Not for me. My family is atheist. We just need to say we are married in front of a couple witnesses." She looked around and frowned. "I think they should be Larnagian witnesses."

"Genetically, *we* are Larnagians," Donna pointed out.

"Oh! Good enough then. I, Wani, am married to, um — Ladd, right? I am married to Ladddave."

"I, Dave, am married to Wani." Her father had already told me she couldn't have a family name — until now. "Laddwani."

"Great. Let's eat." She patted her tummy. "The little one is hungry."

"Don't we get to throw rice?" asked Donna. "At least you can kiss the bride, Dave." So I did. Then we didn't throw rice but it was among the things I started to cook up. There's no denying I was the only one who could really cook in our entire troop.

The rest sat around and drank wine or beer. Except Wani and Susan — they had reason not to. "I was wondering," began Susan. "Um, what with being — um, you guys know I'm pregnant, right?" For the most, she got blank looks. "Oh, I guess not. Well, I am, so that's that." She rushed on. "This whole thing about not teleporting with an unborn child. Ah, there is a chance mine will be — well, you know."

"Able to jump," I said.

"Yeah, that. So, is it dangerous to be on a ship that jumps? I mean, you haven't been worried about it, Wani."

Wani seemed perplexed about coming up with an answer. I

think she had simply been told that some ways of doing things were safe and some weren't, without much explanation.

So the doctor jumped in. "A navigator is not teleporting the ship nor teleporting anyone on it. The ship's computers are able to follow when she jumps. It's like falling through a hole the navigator has made."

"So it doesn't effect people the same way?" I asked.

"That is how it seems. We only have theories about how it actually works, I shall admit."

"Maybe someday," said Donna, "you'll have machines smart enough to do it on their own and all the Larnagians will be out of a job."

I suspected there had been plenty of research done in that direction. Just figuring out how to follow a Larnagian would have been a pretty huge accomplishment.

Wani was staring at Susan. "Is it my father's baby?" she asked.

"It is." It was hard to read Susan's expression. She reached down and scratched Doo behind the ears. "Your brother or sister."

"Will you marry Daddy?"

Susan shook her head. "Not a good idea. Not at all."

The captain's voice broke in. "The Fleet Commander will be shuttling over shortly," it informed us. "She'll want to see you all before Nagudagdag arrives."

"And when Nagudagdag arrives?" I asked.

"That," it replied, "will be up to the Commander."

# Chapter 34

OUTSIDE OF LARNAGIANS, Zyzzuz was the most humanoid alien I had seen so far. She only came up to my waist. Her mouth was wide and rather lizard-like. The Fleet Commander's coverall hid most other details of her anatomy from me.

Including the fact that she was female. I had to take the captain's word for that.

"This is Nagudagdag's daughter?" were her first words to us.

I answered before anyone else could. "She is. And my wife."

"He is aware of this?"

"Not yet," admitted Wani. "As soon as he gets here."

"Perhaps it would be best to get that out of the way immediately," Nok put in.

"Perhaps," replied the commander. She turned back to me. "We may need you to act as courier to the Council." It wasn't a request nor was it an order.

"I can do that too," said Mickie.

"Very well. Do you all understand the situation?" She lifted herself into one of the chairs — designed with Larnagians in mind — and perched there.

We looked at each other. "Some," I told her.

"Our analysis is that Nagudagdag is attempting to establish Ganc's independence from Larnag."

"Wait," said Susan. "Larnag rules Ganc?"

"Perhaps I could fill them in on the background, Commander," offered Nok.

"Do."

"Very well. The Larnagians," he began. "Those on Larnag, that is, have a loose confederation of tribal and semi-feudal governments. They claim to have dominion over Ganc and the leaders on Ganc are just as adamant that they are independent.

Mostly they just posture at each other and have done so for generations."

"So taking control of Paradise strengthens their bargaining position?" asked Donna.

"If they could have maintained that control," Zyzzuz said. "They have already lost it."

I wasn't so sure of that. "It gives us a strong bargaining position now." Whoever 'us' was.

"A stronger one, to be sure," said Nok. "The Council has made no decision on ownership, have they?"

"None," the commander answered. "But the discoverer certainly would have the best claim. That," she said, addressing me, "is why you are here, Dave Ladd, and should take part in any negotiations."

Not that they could keep me out. "What of Larnag then?" I asked. "Will they attempt to gain control here?"

"One of their ships showed up and jumped away again when it saw the fleet," she informed us. "We can assume individual scouts have teleported in to the planet from time to time as well. It is most unlikely they shall attempt to oppose us here."

The captains voice interrupted us. "Nagudagdag is ready to come up. Shall I instruct him to teleport to the lab?"

"Yes, Captain. That would be fine," the commander responded. "He did request that all of you be here," she said to us, "but I do not think you should all take part in any formal negotiations. That is for Dave."

"We are all involved in this," I said. "Mickie, especially." After all, she had done her part in bringing Dagdag to the bargaining table — or wherever aliens bargained.

Whatever comment Commander Zyzzuz might have had on this was forestalled by the materialization of Nagudagdag.

"Dave!" he roared out. "I have heard of your heroic jumps! And yours, Mickie Vogel!" He turned to his daughter. "You have chosen a worthy mate, Wani."

"I married him a few minutes ago."

"Good, good! Now we must find a male good enough for Mickie. I greet you, Commander Zyzzuz. I greet all of you."

I was relieved the big guy approved of our marriage. For all I knew, he might have seen me as an enemy. Now we had to see if we could work together and come up with an agreement for the planet below us, and maybe for the one where I was born.

I'd decided Dagdag's whole plan for seizing Paradise was pretty half-assed but then realized he didn't truly risk much. Maybe it was smart for him to take a shot at it. Be that as it may, we had the upper hand now.

"You should have taken my suggestion of sharing Paradise," I told him outright. I wanted to get to it. I'm pretty sure Zyzzuz disapproved. I'm absolutely sure Nok did. Too bad.

"And I would have shared it," the Larnagian said.

"But you wanted to be in a better position first."

He laughed loudly. "It is so! Now you are in the better position. What will you do, Dave?"

"We'll do something." I was cutting the Connection right out of this conversation, wasn't I? "I'm more concerned about Earth right now."

"Yes, Earth," spoke the commander. "We must know your intentions there, and those of Larnag."

Dagdag shrugged. "I had and have no intentions. As for Larnag, who can say?"

"I can," said Muca, who had suddenly appeared among us.

# Chapter 35

WANI LOOKED LIKE she was ready to commit murder.

"What have you to say?" asked Zyzzuz. "Do you speak for Larnag?"

"I do not. I've had it with those idiots."

"Gu'ursatlag?" asked Nagudagdag.

"That's the one," she replied, more than a little scornfully. "I didn't know he was going to be so stupid."

"Never overestimate your friends," said Susan, "nor underestimate your enemies."

"That is good!" Dagdag said. "I must remember it! Um, how are you, Susan?"

"Pregnant."

That shut the Larnagian up momentarily. Muca continued with her explanations. "You know I jumped to Wani's father when I first found her. That was all it was about then, just letting him know." She turned to her one-time friend. "He was very worried about you."

Wani nodded but said nothing.

"I knew it might end my career as a navigator but — but I thought it was my duty. I couldn't go requesting another post right away, that was for sure! Not after deserting."

"I promised you would always have a place on a Larnagian ship," Dagdag slipped in here.

Muca didn't comment on this but I could see she thought it was a step down. Navigators for the Connected Systems were surely at the top, the best of all those who could move among the worlds.

"I was left idle. That was when Gu'ursatlag contacted me."

Nok felt he should let us know, "Gu'ursatlag is the top leader on Larnag."

"And my enemy," growled Nagudagdag.

"Enemy?" wondered Muca. "Opponent is more accurate. You males are always so dramatic."

"Please continue," requested Zyzzuz. She swung her rather large, bare and somewhat greenish feet back and forth a couple times. The commander was getting tired of inaction.

"Very well. Gu'ur had heard rumors and was curious about the secrecy concerning this planet we had visited. Earth. So he invited me to his clan house and asked me about it. By the way, it's nicer than yours, Nagu."

Surprisingly, Nagudagdag only chuckled at this. Zyzzuz, however, glared at the girl. "Stay on track, please," she said.

"What it came to was that I had little to tell him but knew how to learn more. I offered to do just that and he accepted. Made me some big promises too, you can be sure!"

"Or you made sure," I said. "We needn't know what they were." I was growing impatient too.

She smiled and shrugged. "I wasn't at all certain I could deliver what I promised but I figured I might as well try. You know what I did then. I jumped to the ship above Earth, hid and waited, just in hope you'd show up. And you did! I teleported aboard this ship, accessed the records, copied them, jumped back to Larnag. But I did, ah, make sure to peek at them myself. They were very interesting." Muca giggled. "I had to explain them to Gu'ursatlag."

"So he and his followers know about Earth and its people's abilities," said Commander Zyzzuz.

"And also about Planet Dave," Muca told her. "That was in the records."

"We call it Paradise now. He probed here but nothing more."

"Yes, the Larnagians saw it was too well defended so Gu'ur went to a different plan. He intends to attack Earth and remove it as a threat. Even now, he is putting together a fleet — small compared to this one — and teaching the way to the planet to more and more of his followers."

"Just what we wanted to prevent," I sighed.

The commander had something more useful to say. "Why?" she asked. "What does he hope to accomplish?"

Muca tipped her head as if she were explaining something to one slow-witted. She probably had lots of practice on Larnag. "Why, to prevent humans from coming to take possession of Paradise, as you name it. He believes Nagu here has allied with them and is going to establish a colony." She smiled knowingly. "With the Connection's approval, of course."

There might actually be some truth behind that, and she knew it.

The commander slid down from her seat. "How shall we prevent this? We have a fleet of ships that are useless without navigators."

"Then we will navigate for you," said Dagdag. "I shall go down at once and arrange things." He disappeared without further word.

Zyzzuz turned to the girl. "For your service I shall recommend you be reinstated as a navigator. I am returning to my ship, Captain," she said, speaking to the ceiling and heading out the door.

"Very well, Commander," came the captain's response. It had undoubtedly listened to everything.

What now? I was standing there, staring at those who remained. Wani and Muca were eyeing each other warily, when Doo ambled over. Both were petting him a few seconds later.

Squid sidled close and whispered, "I do wish we'd spent more time with Muca when she navigated this ship. She is undoubtedly the most intelligent Larnagian I've ever encountered."

I could agree. Even on Earth, she'd be considered smart. Muca was indeed a genius among Larnagians. "I wonder just what she was promised for her spy work."

"Marriage, most likely," felt Nok, who had joined us. "To the most powerful male on Larnag. But I think she decided against that."

"So do I," I answered. "And I think Gu'ursatlag dodged a bullet."

# Chapter 36

"MY MEN WILL be teleporting aboard, one by one," Dagdag announced. "Then we can go. Who is navigating?"

"I shall," announced Muca. "Nagudagdag — if I may?"

He squinted at her from beneath his heavy brows. I don't think Dagdag quite trusted her yet and I did not blame him. "Yes?"

"If your men each first visit the ship they will navigate it will make the jump back easier."

He slowly nodded. "You are right. I shall so order." He disappeared again.

The captain sighed. "We could have radioed them."

What we were doing was simple enough — once it was explained to me, Wani and Muca taking turns. It seemed that their enmity had disappeared. I might still warn my wife not to trust her too much, later on.

We need only jump with a shipload of Larnagians to show them where Earth was and then they could immediately jump back and navigate the other ships. The whole fleet would be at Earth in no time to deter Gu'ursatlag. If we could ever get going.

I was impatient, knowing we were near an end to all this. I wanted to be done with the old, to start the new. So what if I had no idea what was involved in making a planet habitable! I'd figure it out. We'd figure it out, a handful of Earth humans and Larnagians.

I did hope those three humans would remain. Donna and Mickie, Susan. For their own sakes, not mine. There was nothing about me to make them want to stay. I can be a bit abrasive. I know this. It has helped neither my career nor my personal relationships. Too wrapped up in myself too, maybe.

Larnagians started showing up on board. Most of them were congregated in the saucer bay but there were a few outliers, teleporters who ended up in crew cabins or utility closets. These were guided to their comrades. They did tend to be big guys, on the whole, though some were no taller than me.

Most just sat down and rested. They had already jumped twice and knew they faced two longer jumps shortly. A big view screen was turned on so they could see Earth as soon as we arrived, get their bearings, and teleport out. "Windows would be better," Wani confided in me. "Especially for these males. They're not so good at orienting themselves." Then she whispered, her voice small and sad. "Some will miscalculate their jump back and be lost."

"But they'll jump anyway," I stated. So would many men on Earth, faced with the same circumstances. I'm not sure I would. "It's time you went to your quarters."

This had been agreed. Indeed, I would have preferred that Wani be left on the planet, as well as our three human women. I hadn't seen Dagdag speak with Susan yet. He might be waiting till all this was over.

Some personnel not needed aboard had been shuttled down to Paradise, to the small camp established there. Then everyone was aboard that needed to be aboard and everyone was off that needed to be off. It was time to go, to jump to Earth, and finish this.

I was in the lab when we jumped. I didn't know we jumped, of course. One couldn't feel it. The captain announced our arrival. All those Larnagians would begin teleporting back to Paradise, back to the fleet, as soon as they felt themselves ready. A few foolish ones would before they felt ready. There are always some like that.

"Pour me another," I asked Squid, "and I'll drink to our success." Then we would have to get involved in whatever was going to happen. It poured me out a rather large beaker of single-malt scotch.

"Dave, could you come to the control center please?" came the captain's voice. "Ah, all of you might as well."

"I reckon I'll save this for later," I said, taking one sip and setting the whiskey aside. "Let's see what it wants."

The captain awaited us and, of course, Muca, still in the navigation chair. "Good," she said. "You take over, Ladd. In case we have to make an emergency jump." She climbed out.

"Why not? It's good to be of some use." I settled into the couch. "Do you expect any emergencies, Captain?"

"There are several Larnagian ships out there," it responded. "And they are, of course, full of Larnagians. We can expect visitors sooner or later."

"So why don't we just jump away and let the fleet take care of them?" I asked. The other ships should be along pretty quickly, as soon as all those navigators got themselves ready to teleport again.

"Our orders were to allow Gu'ursatlag to make contact, if he wished, and begin negotiations," said Nok.

Squid whistled. "And perhaps distract him before the fleet starts showing up."

I could only nod. It made sense of a sort. I did wish Dagdag had remained on board instead of insisting on being one of the navigators. And remained on board with at least a couple of his burly Larnagians, too.

It didn't take long. A big — and somewhat fat — Larnagian male appeared in the control room. Good accurate jump, I had to admit to myself. He had a long unkempt beard hanging onto his chest. "Ah, Muca," he said. "Very good! You have brought them right to us."

The girl smirked. "Sure, Satlag. You didn't think I deserted you, now did you?" I don't think he caught the sarcasm in her voice at all.

"And you shall be rewarded," he said, and turned to the captain. "My men will be teleporting aboard, here and there. We mean you no harm."

"Then what do you mean?" I asked.

He scowled at me. There was definite menace in the scowl. "You're one of *them*, aren't you?"

"He's the one who found the planet," Muca informed him. "They've named it Paradise now."

"Ah! I have heard of your jump. A great feat, Ladd of Earth. But we will have that planet — or take the one now below us."

"There are a few billion of us down there to prevent you."

He didn't seem concerned about that, holding up a broad palm in dismissal. "We have weapons that can remove them. It might be best to do that anyway, and have both worlds!"

Whether Gu'ursatlag bluffed or was serious, I did not know. I did know he was dangerous.

Something buzzed. "What is it?" asked the Larnagian. "Are my men in place?"

A voice came from somewhere in the vicinity of his torso. He must have a communication device on that broad belt around his broad waist. "Ships arriving," it said. "Lots of ships."

Gu'ursatlag turned a snarling face to Muca. "Traitor!"

"Did you really think I'd go along with such a stupid idea?" she asked and then immediately added, "Of course you did. You're just as stupid."

I wasn't sure what this big enraged Larnagian might do. I was ready to transpose myself between him and the girl. He might stumble over me or something. Fortunately, Nagudagdag decided to teleport in right then.

The two males stood there, glowering at each other. From their postures, I expected a physical fight to erupt any second.

No, Nagudagdag knew he had already won, and relaxed. "You are beaten, Gu'ur."

His opponent sagged. He knew it too. "Why are you helping them, Nagu? They are a danger to both of us."

"I have decided they are better friends than they are enemies. We must learn to work with them." That was honest-to-god wisdom. I wondered if someone had whispered it in his ear, not that Dagdag couldn't come up with something like that on his own. I've said before he was smart, as Larnagians go.

"The Fleet Commander will be shuttling over shortly," Captain Squid announced. "Then we can begin our negotiations. Why don't you escort our guests down to the saucer bay, Dave?"

"Will do," I replied. I noted that Nok and Doc remained behind. They and the captain might have things to discuss. It didn't bother me to be left out. Muca followed along behind us.

"It might be best," I told them, "if neither of you had any men aboard this vessel. You are here to negotiate, not to fight."

Gu'ur gave me a sour look, but got on his communicator and ordered his followers to leave. Not that those Larnagians couldn't jump right back on at any time. I assumed Nagudagdag hadn't brought any aboard.

But they, too, would be poised to teleport if called. We could have a pitched battle erupt in the space of a few seconds. The commander's shuttle reached the bay before we did. "Where's the best room for our conference?" she asked at once.

"Will the lab do?" She had been there, after all, and it was a large open room.

"It should." She led the way, the Larnagians close behind, occasionally giving each other threatening glances. Muca and I brought up the rear. The girl seemed quite cheerful.

It did surprise me some that Zyzzuz had no guards. Maybe she felt it best to show trust. I'd say trust is good but caution is better.

Nok and Squid were both there waiting, apparently having been informed the lab was our destination. No one else. "I want my daughter here," growled Dagdag. "Susan too."

"They are not needed," was the commander's response. "Nor are you," she said to Muca. "Please return to the captain, in case he needs you." In case there was a reason to suddenly jump away from here.

I suspected Zyzzuz was primarily exerting her authority at the beginning of the negotiations, showing these two feuding Larnagians she was in charge. It would have done no harm to let others in. Muca was reluctant but did as asked. She would have loved to stay and observe. Of that I had not the least doubt.

Fleet Commander Zyzzuz climbed into one of the chairs, as before, hesitated there only a moment, and then stepped up onto the table. She intended to be on a level with us. But she still looked a little silly when she sat down with her legs dangling over the edge.

"Let us begin," she said.

# Chapter 37

"WE CAN WITHHOLD our navigators," Gu'ursatlag warned.

The commander was not concerned. "An inconvenience, temporary only. Ganc can provide some. Earth can provide many with a little training."

"So you would open Earth up?" asked Nagudagdag. He didn't seem any more comfortable with the idea than his rival. "Bring it into the Connected Systems?"

"We might," she said. "Will it be necessary?"

"Not if you two are willing to cooperate," I told them.

Zyzzuz nodded. "Exactly."

Gu'ursatlag looked thoughtful. Or puzzled. It was hard to be certain. "Then what would be done about Earth?" He gave me a sidelong look. "And those who come from there."

"They would have to be brought into the Connection eventually," said Nagudagdag. "We need to be given time to prepare."

"As would Earth," I said. "It would not do at all for unready humans to start leaping out into the universe. Even I can see that."

"Then you might approve of an agreement to keep Earth shut off for a while?" asked Zyzzuz. Both Larnagians nodded.

"A quarantine," said Gu'ur.

"To keep both sides safe," agreed Nagu.

"And in the meanwhile," I said, "both humans and Larnagians can settle on Planet Dave." I wanted to call it that once more before it officially became Paradise.

"How many humans?" asked Gu'ursatlag at once.

"The four here, to begin with," the commander told him. "Beyond that? You can work that out yourselves, perhaps, but I would advise bringing more and teaching them. Make them ready for the day Earth is opened up."

Nagudagdag pondered that. "It is a good idea," he decided. "How long?"

"Twenty of their years, maybe?" suggested Zyzzuz.

"And a guarantee of twenty more if we feel they are not ready yet," Gu'ursatlag put in. He wasn't as much of a dummy as first impressions had suggested. How could he be and rise to his position on Larnag?

"Very well," agreed the commander. "It shall be put into the treaty. I have complete authority to approve any agreement in the name of the Connected Systems. Now you understand that you and your people will not be allowed to visit Earth?"

"We do," agreed Gu'ur. Nagudagdag nodded as well.

"But," she continued, "that prohibition does not apply to those who are human. Those who come from Earth."

"What of their descendants?" I asked.

"Hmm, that is something I honestly hadn't considered, Dave Ladd. Shall they be allowed to teleport to Earth?"

"Why not?" asked Dagdag.

"I think it might be necessary," added Gu'ursatlag. "They will want to bring more humans. Mates maybe?" He gave me a look. "You will have to control it."

Me? "I'm not in charge," I objected.

"But you must be," Zyzzuz told me. "Do you not agree?" she asked the Larnagians.

"Yes," said Nagudagdag. "Dave will be the leader on Paradise."

"With your daughter beside him?" asked Gu'ursatlag. He actually managed to put some sarcasm into his voice.

"Her loyalty will be to her husband."

"Oh. Married?" Gu'ur actually gave me a rather friendly look. A first! "My congratulations, Dave."

"Then we are all agreed," stated Fleet Commander Zyzzuz. "The rest is details. Please voice your approvals for the record."

"I approve," said Nagudagdag.

"I approve," repeated Gu'ursatlag.

"And you, Dave Ladd? You are part of this."

I kept myself from shrugging. "I approve."

"And I, Zyzzuz approve on behalf of the Connected Systems. I shall return to my ship now. I strongly suggest you have a party." With that, she jumped down from the table and left us.

"A party is a most excellent idea," said Doc Squid. It and Nok had been silent observers, for the most part, through our meeting.

"We must invite the other humans," Nok told us. "Why don't you all come to the lab? I assume you have been watching."

Yeah, they would have. "Muca, too," I added, "if the captain doesn't need her anymore."

It didn't take them long. I think Wani and the three Earth women — and Doo — must have all been together. Muca was only seconds behind them. "I suppose the supply of Earth booze will dry up now," sighed Squid. "What a great opportunity it might have been!"

"I promise to pop home and fetch you a bottle now and again," I told him. "Or maybe set up a distillery on Paradise. Yes —" I could see it already. Paradise Bourbon, the best in the Connected Systems!

"You will have to plant the proper grains first," Nok pointed out. "It will be a big job, Dave."

"Wani and I can handle it," I assured him. After a couple drinks I was willing to assure anything.

"We'll help," Mickie said. "Donna and me. We're not going back to Earth."

Donna nodded her agreement. "Mickie is going to write a book all about this for those on Earth to read someday."

"In Alienese?" I asked.

Mickie laughed. "That might be best!"

Meanwhile, Nagudagdag was mooning about something. Oh, not something. I knew very well that Susan was on his mind.

He eventually got up his nerve to say, "Susan, will you marry me and come live on Ganc?"

She didn't hesitate in her answer. "I think not, Daggy. I've decided to live on Paradise, too." There was a hint of a snicker. "If Dave can put up with me on the same planet. Of course, I expect you to visit me and our child."

Dagdag looked a little crestfallen but I reckoned he would get over it.

"I, too, have offered marriage to someone," Gu'ursatlag said. I think the liquor had gotten to him some also. He turned to Muca. "Though you twisted things to your own ends, they came out well. I would still be willing to make you my wife."

"No need to keep your promise. I think I want a smart Earth guy like Wani has." She turned to my wife. "Can we go find one?"

"Sure," came the reply, "but he'll never be as good as mine."

I probably should have blushed.

# Chapter 38

WE FLOATED ABOVE Paradise.

"I think a little more temperate spot would be good," I said. "It was pretty tropical where camp was set up."

"As long as there isn't snow," said Mickie. I was completely in agreement there.

"We'll have to go back, those of us who can, and tie up things at home. I can take you, Susan, after the kid arrives."

"Right. I have more banjos at home that need to come here. And we need a bitch for Doo or we'll run out of dogs pretty quick."

Doo raised no objections to this plan.

"I can run you home if you want," Mickie told Donna. "I guess we both have relatives we should let know we're alive."

They both seemed okay with the idea of living on Paradise, of living with each other. All we had gone through seemed to have brought them closer. Probably okay with having children, too, when things were settled. That would happen if it happened.

We had other children to be concerned about, Wani's, Susan's. The first newborn humans on this world. The first of many. It wouldn't be long now for Wani and mine. We just might have a wedding later with a priestess, too, whatever Wani's religious beliefs — or lack thereof — might be. This was going to a Larnagian world as much as a human one.

Larnagians would come, from Larnag, from Ganc. And Mickie and I, and then others, could start bringing people here from Earth, a few at a time. People who wanted and needed a new life. They didn't have to be able to teleport.

Of course, we Earthlings would soon become the senior partners, simply because we were smarter. Who knows, maybe Wani and I were the start of something that would become common and a merged people would result.

When Earth was told of us some day, we would be ready, we exiled humans, the Larnagians, the whole of the Connected Systems. I would be old by then. Gone maybe.

But Paradise would be there, waiting for them.

www.ingramcontent.com/pod-product-compliance
Lightning Source LLC
Chambersburg PA
CBHW031113260626
47172CB00001B/344